PRAISE FOR *MUNRO VS. THE COYOTE*

"Groth introduces readers to a sympathetic main character who is trying to move through trauma and to a sparkling supporting cast that gives voice to disability... [Munro's] first-person narration is strong (both sassy and heart-wrenching) and the thoughtful handling of trauma and difference, both genuine and relevant. Characters that will steal readers' hearts with their humor and resilience, smooth writing, and a satisfying and hopeful ending make this a book to enjoy both emotionally and critically."

—*Kirkus Reviews*

"*Munro vs. the Coyote* is engrossing, entertaining and uplifting...This book will strike a chord and shift perspectives for many readers while it entertains them. Highly Recommended."

—*CM Magazine*

"A great tale about friendship and open-mindedness, and accepting differences in others."

—Susin Nielsen,
award-winning author of *Optimists Die First*

"A celebration of all that makes us weird, wonderful, and unique. Groth creates characters who learn resilience in the face of grief and discrimination and does it with the perfect balance of humor and heart."

—Eileen Cook,
bestselling author of *With Malice*

"In addition to some laugh-out-loud humour, this page-turner has some heart-wrenching moments...It is a richly layered book about love, the tenacity of the human spirit, and our capacity to mend. Darren Groth is a brilliant storyteller...This book was a delight to review."

—*The Ormsby Review*

MUNRO VS. THE COYOTE

DARREN GROTH

ORCA BOOK PUBLISHERS

Library and Archives Canada Cataloguing in Publication

Groth, Darren, 1969–, author
Munro vs. the coyote / Darren Groth.

Issued in print and electronic formats.
ISBN 978-1-4598-1409-7 (hardcover).—ISBN 978-1-4598-1410-3 (pdf).—
ISBN 978-1-4598-1411-0 (epub)

I. Title. II. Title: Munro versus the coyote.
PS8613.R698M86 2017   jc813'.6   c2017-900848-x
c2017-900849-8

First published in the United States, 2017
Library of Congress Control Number: 2017932501

Summary: In this novel for teens, Munro Maddux goes to Australia on a student exchange in order to try and deal with his younger sister's death.

Orca Book Publishers is dedicated to preserving the environment and has printed this book on Forest Stewardship Council® certified paper.

Orca Book Publishers gratefully acknowledges the support for its publishing programs provided by the following agencies: the Government of Canada through the Canada Book Fund and the Canada Council for the Arts, and the Province of British Columbia through the BC Arts Council and the Book Publishing Tax Credit.

Cover illustration by Robert John Paterson
Edited by Sarah Harvey
Cover design by Rachel Page
Author photo by Lauren White

ORCA BOOK PUBLISHERS
www.orcabook.com

Printed and bound in Canada.

20   19   18   17   •   4   3   2   1

For W, C, J and especially for Mum, Dad and my two brothers, who were meant to be my sisters.

And all people live, not by reason of any care
they have for themselves, but by the love
for them that is in other people.

LEO TOLSTOY

BRISBANE

Have you always wanted to travel to other FAB parts of the world?

Not so much.

Do you want to immerse yourself in an AWESOME new culture?

If it helps.

Are you ready for the RAD adventure you've always dreamt about?

Not my dream.

Then YOU are srsly the sort of student **YOLO** *Canada is looking for!*

I srsly doubt it.

I shut the handbook, turn it over so I don't have to look at the title on the front page—*Munro Maddux, You Da Man!*—and stuff it back in my carry-on. A horn sounds. The baggage carousel grinds into motion. Passengers from my flight push forward, hoping their bags will be the first to appear. There's plenty of chatter around me.

"Can you believe we're here?"

"I can't wait to go to the beach!"

"Do you think there'll be kangaroos hopping down our street?"

Most of these people are too old or too young to be on a student exchange. Still, they're the ones who should be reading the YOLO handbook. These are YOLO-type folk. Loud. Lame. Memes-in-waiting.

YOLO. Worst name ever. My parents wanted to go with a more established agency—YES or Youth for Understanding or ASSE. All three showed me the hand when my tenth-grade report card hit their application inboxes. So YOLO it was. I figured an organization that had a god-awful name wouldn't be too picky about their candidates. I was right. Their selection criteria— which included *Student motivation and commitment must be to the MAX!* and *Student academic grade level must be a WICKED B AVERAGE!*—turned out to be more of a wish list than a hard line. They didn't seem to care that my marks were less than a *WICKED B AVERAGE!* or that my application essay asked if they'd be open to a bribe.

Maybe they took pity on me after Mom's email about Evie.

Whatever.

My suitcase eases up the conveyor belt and tumbles down onto the carousel. The ruby-red ribbon on the handle flutters like a flag in the wind. I heave the bag off the roundabout, then untie the ribbon and hold it in my hand.

Here we are, Evie. Where you always wanted to be.

I stuff the ribbon in my carry-on, along with the YOLO handbook. Friggin' YOLO. You only live once? Total BS. Some people don't get to live at all.

The pickup guy is waiting for me in the terminal. He holds a sign that reads *MUNRO MADDUX, YEAH!* For a second I consider ditching him to hitch a ride.

"Welcome to Brisbane!" he says, presenting a fist. I hesitate, then give it a gentle bump. "I'm Lars, and this is the beginning of six months that will change you forever!"

"Here's hoping, Lars."

"Hey, you can call me Lars And In Charge." He snorts and gives a time-out sign. "Just kidding! You don't have to call me that. I'm here to take you to your host family!"

I don't know what I was expecting when I touched down in Brisbane, but I can say with some level of confidence that it wasn't Lars. For starters, he's not an Aussie. He's Canadian, sounds like he grew up out east, probably Toronto. He's also...well, *old*. Thinning hair. Bit of a gut. Gray in the stubble. He looks like one of Dad's poker buddies.

We walk to the parking lot. Lars lays out a Wikipedia of factoids: the blistering sun, the crazy traffic, the current cricket match, cockatoos, thunderstorms, the sun again, water restrictions, skin cancer, the long sleeves and broad-brimmed hats that are stock summer wear. His first question comes after we've hit the road in his steam room of a car.

"What you got there, Munro, if you don't mind me asking?"

I do mind, but I'm sure Lars minds that I'm reading instead of staring wide-eyed and openmouthed out of the window.

"Info package," I reply. "For my new school. Sussex State High."

"Ah, very good! Although I'm guessing you probably already read it cover to cover on the way over."

I shake my head. "Didn't get a chance."

"Oh?"

"Flight was only fifteen hours."

He squirms in his seat and hits the AM button on the dash. A nasally talk-show guy punches through the airwaves. He's got a bug up his butt about "illegals." Lars switches to a station playing *The Nineties at Nine* and holds up a hand in apology. I nod.

"That dude is soooo un-YOLO," I say. "Am I right?"

Lars smiles thinly into the rearview mirror.

With some band called Regurgitator and its catchy song "Polyester Girl" providing the soundtrack, I return to the Sussex info package. The big thing that jumps off the pages: the formal uniform. I've seen it before, but it's for real now that I'm in Australia. Pants, shirt, tie. Pleated skirts for the girls. The getup is *strongly encouraged on Wednesdays*; the rest of the week you can wear the sports uniform.

The package has other nuggets of info about the school. Its motto is *Climb the Highest Peak*. I Google Earth-ed Brisbane's highest peak, Mount Coot-tha, a while back—it's like the bunny hill on Cypress Bowl. Climbing that should be a breeze. The sports lineup includes *Boys' Touch* and *Girls' Touch*. I'm not sure which one to sign up for. One of the electives is *Tourism*. The ski trip is in July. The school is big on volunteering.

Overall, I can't say I'm looking forward to being a student at Sussex State High. But I don't have zero desire to show either.

That's a big improvement.

Over Christmas, four months into eleventh grade, nine months after Evie's death, I was done with school. I didn't hate it—I just couldn't function anymore. The people at Delta Secondary School weren't to blame. They had found a way through their grief, planting a cherry blossom by the admin block, printing a special *We will remember you forever* newsletter with dozens of kind quotes, flying the BC flag at half-mast. Hundreds turned up to her funeral. It was helpful for everyone.

Everyone except me.

I had flashbacks. Chest pains. My right hand ached constantly. I got angry at other students walking too slow or brushing my shoulder or giving any hint of side-eye. And there was a voice. The Coyote, my therapist, Ollie, called it. Teasing, taunting. Barking. Sometimes biting. It played at being people I knew—teachers and students, friends and relatives. Even Mom and Dad from time to time. That was the worst. Four months into grade eleven, I was hearing the Coyote everywhere in school, not just on the stretch of corridor between the library and Mrs. Bouchard's room. My problem had become something central, at the very core of my being. And it wouldn't matter if I moved to Burnsview or Seaquam or Sands—the Coyote would follow.

On New Year's Day, I straight up told Mom and Dad I wanted out of school. *For how long?* they asked.

I said I didn't know. They balked. I pleaded. They reasoned. I resisted. They sympathized. I punched a wall. Alternatives were proposed and rejected. Homeschooling was an added pressure none of us could handle. Distance learning was, in Mom's eyes, a "pretend education."

How about you work with us for a bit? Dad suggested. *Just until you figure things out.*

I couldn't do it. The Evelyn Maddux Foundation was a great thing for sure. In just seven and a half months, it had raised over 150 grand for Down syndrome awareness and research. More important, it was Mom and Dad's rehab, their way of keeping Evie's memory alive. It would never be that for me. Seeing the name Evelyn Maddux every day, hearing it spoken out loud, selling ribbons and buttons and bracelets that only existed because she was no longer with us…compared to that, school was a breeze.

Around sunset, with heavy clouds hinting at a snowy start to the new year, Mom stumbled upon a possibility with promise: *What about a student exchange?*

My first thought was, What good would that do? But over the next couple of days, the idea persisted. Then it grew on me. Then it grew around me. Ollie told me in every therapy session that the flashbacks, the physical symptoms, the bad associations, the loss of connection to others, the Coyote…recovering from all of it started with *finding a place for it to go.* Could that

7

place be a country? And not just any country—the one that was Evie's obsession?

I wonder if Mr. Adams is here. Maybe I'll run into him. That would be some serious coincidence. Population of Brisbane's only about, oh, two million.

I wonder if he still remembers you, Evie. For sure he must. The eleven-year-old you. That's the age you'll always be to him. He's lucky to remember you like that.

Thirteen years, four months, eight days—that's the age you'll always be to me.

Australia. Home of Mr. Adams, Evie's sixth-grade teacher. He told me once that he saw school as the sky and his students as stars. And Evie shone brightest. In his class she learned to swim and put up a tent and cook a dessert called pavlova and throw a rugby pass like a seasoned pro. The inspiration of Mr. Adams soon became the aspiration of Evelyn Maddux. She planned to visit his home state of Queensland. She imagined holding a koala and playing a didgeridoo, running on a beach where the white sand squeaked under her feet. She loved Chris Hemsworth and was determined to marry him. She made plane tickets out of cardboard and crayon. She searched online for houses for sale in suburban Brisbane. The dream of Australia gave her purpose and filled up her heart.

It wouldn't stay filled. The hole between her ventricles made sure of that.

The car slows. Lars flips the indicator and turns in to a short driveway that fronts a beige house with pine-green trim. Two flags, side by side—one Canadian, one Australian—are tied to the top railing of the front patio. An old bedsheet is suspended underneath, the words MUNRO, WELCOME TO AUSTRALIA, MATE! in blue spray paint. Lars parks behind a car that looks a bit like a Mustang, cuts the engine and *pip-pips* the horn. He turns, forearm propped on the passenger seat.

"Your host family awaits your pleasure, Master Maddux."

·············●············

On the YOLO Canada website, there's a series of short videos about past exchanges. Each one is a softball lobbed toward home plate, all joy and laughter and zit-free faces and *This is the greatest thing ever!* and *How can I possibly go back home?* They all have over-the-top, lame titles. *On the Streets of Philadelphia. Hungary for Life. Smile and Say Swiss Cheese! Been There, London That!*

No way the videos are legit. The people are real enough, sure, but the bubblegum tone? No doubt there would've been tough times. That's life. That's truth.

And even if the occasional student exchange ends up being a Disney movie, it doesn't mean it will happen to me.

The Hyde family isn't the problem. They're friendly and easygoing. Soon after Lars's departure, and following a quick tour of *chez* Hyde, Mom Nina—a hummingbird with reddish hair and a thing for purple clothes—sent me to bed for a "nana nap" so I could start resetting my body clock. Since I woke up, she's been studying for Munro Maddux 101. What do I like to eat and drink, what are my favorite TV shows, which video games do I play? She writes everything down on an MM list she posts on the fridge.

Dad Geordie's been welcoming in a different way. A big barrel of a "bloke," he introduced himself as Dr. Jekyll and wanted to know if I'd ever come across a grizzly (I said I hadn't and told him I probably wouldn't be talking to him if I had). He shook his head and admitted he couldn't understand why Australia had the reputation of being such a dangerous place when in the True North Strong and Free there were *bears and mountain lions and bloody great moose looking to make a mess of you*. He also warned that any Dad joke I didn't laugh at (*see* Dr. Jekyll) would result in a grounding.

Son Rowan—only child, also in eleventh grade—seems chill. According to Nina, he's a gifted cook, a real chance to get on *MasterChef* one day. According to Rowan, he's a snowboard pro-in-waiting. He's already asked me about Whistler three times. Each time he sounds me out, Nina gets a look on her face like she got caught in the rain wearing socks and sandals. As a team the Hydes seem close, fun, free of the dark clouds that can hang over a family. It's a vibe I haven't encountered in a while.

I hope the Hydes haven't got their hearts set on being in a YOLO video. I'm not like all those made-for-TV teens. I'm a ringer, an outlier. I'm here because my little sister never made it, and I'm stuck with the fallout of her death. I'm the stand-in big brother and the psycho surviving son.

They don't make videos about those guys.

........•.........

"So, Munro," asks Nina, "you're the only child in the Maddux family, hey?"

I steal a glance at the others. Geordie is at the barbecue, squeezing lemon on the barramundi fish he bought especially for my first supper Down Under. Rowan is chest deep in the Jacuzzi, mirrored aviator shades on, Red Bull in hand. Neither looks like he's listening in, but I sense they are.

I shift my feet from the camping chair's footrest and sit up straight. This moment is important. Weighty. They'll be shocked. *Munro had a younger sister and she died at age thirteen* probably wasn't part of their student-exchange binder. So it's up to me to reveal the Maddux dark cloud. And, to be honest, it's okay. I get to tell the story on my terms.

They get the basics. Evie had Down syndrome. She had a ventricular septal defect, a hole in the heart, that was inoperable. It was thought to be low-ish risk, but it didn't turn out that way. Last March she collapsed at school, and efforts to revive her were unsuccessful. She's buried in the Boundary Bay cemetery in Delta.

You left out so much, Munro.

Shut up, Coyote.

A hush creeps in. Only the crackle of the barbecue and the fizz of the Jacuzzi's open vents drift through the space. I have deflections ready—"That's all I want to say...I'm not comfortable talking about it anymore... Leave me the hell alone"—but they remain holstered. Rowan has lifted his shades above his forehead and, with his free hand, is scooping bubbles from the surface of the water. Geordie wipes his hands on his *Licensed to Grill* apron and thuds down in the nearest plastic chair, the onions ignored for a moment. Nina covers her mouth, leans forward and lays a hand on my forearm. There's a tiny tremble in her fingers.

"No doubt your sister's watching over you, Munro," she says. "So we'd better take good care of you."

"Bloody oath," adds Geordie.

Rowan raises his Red Bull. "These two have done an all-right job with me so far."

"Thank you," I say. "I appreciate it."

With that the Hydes slip back into barbecue routine, my dark cloud no longer interrupting their fine weather. Nina tosses the pasta salad and unveils a tasty-looking pie called "Heavenly Tart," which she says was named after her. Geordie starts swearing as he examines the state of the barramundi. Rowan puts his drink and sunglasses aside and announces he's going to breathe underwater by sucking air through the Jacuzzi vents. He drops out of sight.

These people really should demand a refund from YOLO.

...............●...........

Jet lag sets in around 8:00 PM (2:00 AM Vancouver time). Through a series of yawns, I inform the Hydes that I'm heading for bed. Geordie and Rowan wave from the couch.

"You got everything you need?" asks Nina.

"I think so."

"Sorted out the air con in your room?"

"Yes."

"We're thinking tomorrow we might go out for breakfast—there's a great little café that has a 'BrisVegas Mixed Grill' on Saturdays. It's walking distance from here. No pressure. I know you mentioned you do exercises in the morning."

I nod. "Fifty push-ups, a hundred sit-ups."

"Good on you! Okay, maybe we'll see how you feel after that, hey?"

"Sure. Hopefully I'll be on Aussie time after a good night's sleep."

"No worries." She steps forward. I brace for a hug, but it doesn't come. She reaches out, tugs playfully on my Canucks ballcap and smiles.

"We're really glad you're here with us, Munro."

"Me too."

Nina fetches an extra pillow and wishes me a goodnight. Closing the door to my bedroom, I hear Rowan call out, "Don't let the drop bears bite!"

Pre-crash, I check Facebook. There are a ton of notifications, all of them for the status update I posted just before takeoff: *Bye*. One hundred and forty-three Likes, thirty-seven comments. *Have lots of fun! Totally jealous. Why didn't you take me with you?*

"No idea," I murmur.

I close Facebook, go to my mail and click *Compose*. I type in the subject heading *Here Now*.

Hey, Mom and Dad:

Arrived okay. Pickup went fine at Brisbane airport. I'm here with the Hydes—they're cool. We had barbecued barramundi (an Aussie fish) for supper. It tasted great, although it was a bit burnt. The Hydes have promised to take good care of me. School starts Wednesday, day after Australia Day.

Will write again soon.

M

I click *Send* and flick my right hand, trying to shake off the familiar pain bearing down on each and every knuckle.

Are you ever going to tell your mom and dad about me, Munro? About how you talk to me all the time?

You're the one who always starts the talking, Coyote.

You told the counselor about our little chats. But she doesn't know everything.

Ollie knows enough.

Will you share it with anyone in Australia? Maybe the Hydes? Maybe someone at your new school?

No.

So you're never going to tell anyone about how you always talk to me?

No.

How come, Munro?

Because I won't have to!

How come?

Because this is where it ends! Australia! This is where you get off! Okay? When I go back home, I won't have the bad thoughts and the freeze-ups and the pain and the sadness. And I won't have to fucking hear you anymore! I won't!

Climbing into bed, I look around the room that will be my crib until late August.

An Aboriginal painting hangs above the corner desk. It's some sort of lizard done in the sweet dot style I saw once on the Knowledge Network. Surf magazines of varying ages are fanned out on the lowest shelf of the TV stand. A tiny stuffed koala, no bigger than a tennis ball, clings to the stem of the pedestal fan.

I count out five deep breaths and pull the thin sheet up to my neck.

Do you really believe that, Munro? About this ending in Australia?

Yes.

So you want to forget your sister, the person you loved more than anyone in the world? You never want to think about Evie again?

Of course not. I will never forget her, and I will always think about her. I just want to have the good thoughts. And I want to be in control of those thoughts. When, where. Which ones.

You're stuck because of her.

I'm not stuck because of Evie. It's not her fault.

It's my fault.

SUSSEX HIGH

I've seen my share of counselor offices this past year.

This one belongs to Ms. MacGillivray, Sussex guidance officer. It doesn't fit the usual mold. Yes, there are the motivational messages on posters and notepads and screen savers: *Always set the trail, never follow the path*; *Success is a journey, not a destination*; and *Your attitude, not your aptitude, will determine your altitude*. But there's also *Believe in yourself, because the rest of us think you're a tool* and *Everything in life is easier when you know the cheat codes*. Then there's the roller-derby merch and ads, framed Bris-Banshee T-shirts with signatures all over, a maroon helmet with a yellow star on the side. Several framed action pics feature Ms. MacGillivray herself in fluorescent orange skates, busting through a pack in camouflage getup, sitting in the penalty box with arms extended. According to the captions, her derby name is Bail Her Swift.

"First day at Sussex!" she says, elbows resting on her desk. She has a big round yellow bruise on her right arm. "How are you finding it, Munro?"

"Okay so far, Ms. MacGillivray."

"Call me Ms. Mac. Uniform looks great."

"Thanks."

"Bit of a change from the fashion show back home, I imagine."

"I wasn't much of a model anyway."

Ms. Mac smirks and says, "Nice!" I hear it as *noise*. In my short time in Australia, there's been a lot of *noise*.

"Subject selection all right?" she asks.

"I think so."

"Good. Your situation is not that different to the other elevens. You want to take the best possible marks and credits into your final year of secondary school. Your year twelve will be back in Canada, of course, but the subjects are comparable and transferable. We can talk about that a bit more once you're under way, hey?" She takes a sip from a fancy chrome travel mug. "The purpose of this little check-in is much more casual. I'd like to get to know you a tad." She waits, allowing me to fully absorb the statement. I suppress a yawn. "You don't mind?"

"Give 'er."

"What's that?"

"Just a Canadian expression. It means 'go nuts.'"

"Give 'er." Ms. Mac writes it down on a Post-it. "So tell me, you're from Vancouver?"

"Yes."

"Great city. Family?"

"Mom and Dad. Married. To each other."

"Brothers, sisters?"

"No."

"Just you?"

"Just me."

Ms. Mac scribbles another note. I look away. A groundskeeper framed in the window is fertilizing the main courtyard garden.

She'll find out about Evie, Munro.

No she won't.

You've already told the Hydes. They'll tell her.

They don't know squat. And they won't say a word to her or anyone else. I made them promise yesterday, when we were at Kangaroo Point. Nina crossed her heart. Geordie laid his hand on "the Queensland Bible"— a biography of some rugby player called King Wally. Rowan said he'd be far too busy talking about himself.

I think people here should know about her. They should know about what happened. You're treating her like she never existed.

No I'm not.

"Munro. Hey, Munro! You with me?"

"Um, yeah. I'm with you. Sorry about that."

"You okay?"

"I'm fine."

Ms. Mac dips her head to the side, closes an eye, points a finger. She's taking aim with her guidance gun. "You were off with the fairies there."

"Sorry."

"Don't apologize. This is a big change. Six months is a long time to be out of your comfort zone."

I suck in a breath, exhale. "For sure."

"You're in good hands with the Hydes though. They're top shelf. Did Rowan tell you his father's a legend in this town?"

"Uh, no. He didn't."

"I'll let him fill you in."

Ms. MacGillivray says getting to know me a tad has not yet reached a tad, but this is a good moment to inform me about all the "amazing cultural opportunities" at Sussex. Challenges and olympiads, workshops and camps. There is the Computational and Algorithmic Thinking Competition and something else called the

Sleek Geeks Science Eureka Prize. The school has more bands than Coachella. The compulsory volunteering program kicks off next week—"a great chance to do some good for the community and yourself," she assures me.

"Now then," Ms. Mac says. "The sixty-four-thousand-dollar question. What is your *er* word?"

"My *er* word?"

"Yep. What is your *er* word, Munro?" She drums the desk, her short fingernails painted with yellow lightning bolts against a black background. Her smile widens with each passing second. The bruise on her arm is staring at me.

"I'm sorry, Miss…I don't…"

Ms. Mac rises, moves away from the chair, gestures for me to follow. We end up in front of the picture of her in the penalty box, yelling at the unseen ref.

"Every Sussex student should have a goal for the year—well, for you it's six months—and in my experience it helps to attach an *er* word to it. Smarter, happier. Clearer." She points at the picture. "Louder. Whatever *er* word you choose, it should always be in the back of your head, informing everything you do." She holds up a hand. "Now don't feel like you need to come up with your word right this minute. Pretty much every student takes some time to think about it, stew it over, before they come back to me and—"

"I have it, Miss."

"What's that, Munro?"

"I have my *er* word."

Ms. Mac does a double take. "You've got it already? That might be a record." She taps out a brief rhythm on her thigh. "Okay then, hit me."

Can I guess?

No.

Taller?

What did I say?

Super?

Shut up!

It can't be brother.

I flex my right hand.

"*Better* is my word, Miss. I want to be better."

·············●·············

"Ready to meet the gang?" Rowan asks.

"I guess," I reply.

We skirt the library and the art studio. I focus in on the things that distance this school from DSS. Gum trees. Shade tarpaulins. A tribute mural called *Flood Heroes of 2011*. A collection of highway signs that includes *Canberra 1199 km* and *Uluru 2205 km* and *Broome 3320 km*.

"How'd it go with Ms. Mac?"

"You mean Bail Her Swift?"

Rowan turns, eyebrows high on his forehead. "She's got a new derby name? She used to be Kim Karbashian."

"She wanted to get to know me a tad."

"Did she give you the old 'What's your *er* word' speech?"

"Yeah. You've heard it before?"

"We all have." Rowan says hi to a trio of girls. After they pass, I hear murmurings and laughter. One of them says "new talent."

"My *er* word for the year is legendary-er," Rowan says.

"Good word."

We arrive at the soccer field, site of a promised welcome-back lunch for senior students. Five food trucks are parked in a semicircle near the center spot. A few tables, chairs and benches are strewn around, but most of the students are sitting on the grass. We wander toward a group of four—one boy, three girls—occupying the front right corner of the sideline bleachers. They're chowing down like it's the only meal they'll get all year.

"You couldn't wait five minutes for us?" asks Rowan, stealing a pierogi from one of the girls and barely escaping a hand slap.

"We thought you might be bringing your own truck, Chef Row," answers the boy, mouth full of brisket. "Although these are good. And I don't think they're runnin' outta food anytime soon."

"They might if you're here for another half hour," one of the girls says.

"Ha! This coming from Renee Hodges, champ of last year's watermelon-eating contest at the fete!"

"That was a comp—this is real life. Or the buffet, as you call it."

"Can you two get a room?"

"Ew! Maevey! I'm tryin' to eat here!"

"Munro," announces Rowan, "meet the gang. Renee, Caro, Digger and Maeve."

I had hoped "the gang" would resemble the stereotypical Aussies in Whistler—tanned skin, sun-bleached hair, flip-flops, Billabong logos everywhere. Sadly, they're more like my friends in the valley than their mates on the mountain. Maeve reminds me of Darcy, with her selfie-stick limbs and stylish glasses. Renee, sitting cross-legged, both hands on the top knee, back straighter than a prairie highway...she's totally Shawn. Septum ring and all. Digger has Louis's peach fuzz and startled hair. I sigh. It was unfair to expect these strangers to be a postcard just so I could stomach school again. Actually, now that I think about it, Mr. Adams—Evie's idol, the best Australian who ever lived—was bald and round and wore Denver Hayes jeans that sagged in the crotch. Not exactly a poster boy for the Aussie look.

Caro, she's a bit different. *Nuit*, one of a handful of words I remember from ninth-grade French, springs to mind. Night. She's a shadowy figure. Not in a sinister, Madame Hydra sort of way—more just her appearance. She's a collection of dark shades: skin, hair, black-leather wristbands, gray Converse shoes. Her expression, though, is just the opposite, all light and bright. Her eyes are big and wide. Her mouth looks ready to break out in a smile, even when filled with ramen noodles. The stud in her nose glints like shaved ice in the sun.

Rowan hustles me over to the food trucks. After a scan of menus, I go for an Oz burger, which includes a fried egg and beetroot. We head back to the group, and I dig in, trying to give off the vibe of a YOLO video teen.

"I can't wait for *The Addams Family*," says Maeve. "So cool we're doing that for our musical."

"You going to audition?" asks Renee.

"Hells yeah! I want to play Wednesday. If not her, then Morticia."

"As long as it's not Fester."

"Word."

Digger looks toward Rowan and me. "You got any idea what they're talking about?"

"None," replies Rowan, scrutinizing his samosa. "How about you, Renee? What have you got circled on the calendar?"

"Hmm, it's a toss-up between Vaccination Day and the Athletics Carnival."

"Ooh, yeah, tough choice."

"Too tough. And you, Mr. My Kitchen Rules? You counting the days until the Great State High School Cook-Off?"

"Nope. I'm all about the ski trip in July." Rowan spreads his feet, extends his arms and performs a series of gyrations, more hula dance than snowboard shred. "Your turn, Digs. What's your thing this year? Lemme guess—driving your old man's Prius to school?"

Digger shakes his head. "Semiformal. I'm going to have the best date of anyone there." He eyes each one of us in turn before making his announcement. "Jessica Mauboy."

A hush parachutes in. Rowan plays with his phone, then hands it to me. The screen displays Jessica Mauboy's Wikipedia page. Twenty-six. Singer. Songwriter. Actress. Runner-up on *Australian Idol*. Ranked number sixteen on the *Herald Sun*'s list of the 100 greatest Australian singers of all time. The one credit I recognize is her starring role in *The Sapphires*. It was one of many Australian movies Evie tracked down on Netflix. She watched them all at least twice.

"Jessica Mauboy, A-list celeb, and Corey 'Digger' Dulwich, BMX prodigy." Rowan nods slowly, then with more speed. "Why the hell not?"

"Why the hell not!" repeats Maeve.

"I can see it happening," says Caro.

"I think you might be a bit too good for her, but whatever," adds Renee.

The group looks my way. I swallow my final chunk of Oz burger.

"Try not to break her heart, eh?" I say.

Digger bites his bottom lip. His Adam's apple begins to bounce. He gets to his feet, descends the bleachers and jogs over to the food trucks.

"He might be a while," says Rowan. "You're up, Caro."

"Mmm, hard act to follow." Caro shifts into a lotus position on the bench. "What I am looking forward to the most in year eleven...I'd have to say the end." A chorus of groans prompts her to elaborate. "I'm not dreading the year. Totally the opposite, in fact. This year is gonna be great, our best yet. I honestly believe that, and that's why the end is the best part. We'll be more grown up. We'll have learned new things, made new friends." She glances in my direction. "And we'll be doing it together."

Maeve gives Caro's forearm a squeeze. "That's a beautiful speech, babe. You're gonna be an awesome lawyer one day. Don't you agree, Renee?"

"Ha! She said *doing it*."

"There you go. Renee agrees too."

Rowan gestures toward me. "Lucky last, Munro."

I fold my paper plate in half, scan for the nearest bin. "It's okay, man. I'm the newbie. You guys don't want to hear from me."

"Rubbish, mate! You're one of us now! You're wearing our dope uniform. You ate your first Oz burger. You've already had a heart-to-heart with Ms. Mac. Tell us—what are you fired up for?"

I look at the group's expectant faces.

They're all watching, Munro.

Just like at DSS, when the ambulance arrived, when it left.

At the funeral.

Watching.

Thinking.

Don't look at them.

I lower my gaze toward the folded plate balancing on my lap.

"I'm with Caro," I say. "I'm looking forward to the end."

···········●···········

On the train home after school, Rowan slouches in the seat across from me. As we pass through a tunnel, he flips his headphones from his ears to his neck, digs in his back pocket and hands me a folded paper. It's an ad for a place called Liber8.

"One of those escape-room setups," he says. "You get locked away and you've got an hour to use the clues and find a way out. Heard of 'em?"

I nod. "My friend Louis did one in Richmond. It was like an ancient Egyptian tomb or something."

"Sweet. Apparently, this one has an asylum setup like they used to have here in Brissy. I've got some discount passes. Me and the gang are gonna go do it Saturday week. Keen?"

"Um, yeah. Sure."

"Bewdy."

Rowan takes back the paper and returns it to his pocket. His gaze is locked and loaded now, his grin crooked and twitchy, like a liquor-store clerk spying a fake ID.

"You and Caro hit it off, hey?"

"I guess so."

"The two of you had a good chat on the way back from lunch."

"Just sort of happened. I hope I wasn't outta line."

"Nope."

"She wanted to know about Canada."

"She wanted to know about *you*, man."

Rowan removes his headphones, starts winding the cord around the earpieces. "I noticed when Caro asked you about your fam, you said you were an only child."

I pause my game of *Temple Run*. "You caught that, eh?"

"Yeah."

"Thanks for not spilling the beans."

"Hey, they're your beans." Rowan leans forward. "I know you've only just met 'em, but if you did want to tell the gang about your sister, I know they'd be real good about it."

A lull creeps into the conversation. Snippets of chat from neighboring Sussex students find my ears. A hyped guy in the seat behind me is telling friends about a parkour shoot he's planning. The pouty girls across the aisle are comparing "slags" on *The Bachelor*. A younger crew, probably eighth-graders, is discussing *Splatoon* strategy.

"Ms. Mac said your dad is a legend in Brisbane."

Rowan runs a hand down his school tie. "Yeah, he is."

"What did he do...if you're cool with telling me?"

"It's cool. You would've found out soon enough." He shifts his butt back, puts his hands on his knees and brings his feet together. He looks like he's posing for a family photo. "Dad swam out and saved a guy in the Logan River during the 2011 floods. Pulled him out of his car. He was given the Star of Courage and the Queensland Police Service Valour Award, which is the highest honor in the state for a cop."

"I didn't realize he was a policeman."

"Retired in 2014. Permanent medical leave."

I leave a good-sized space for Rowan to continue, but he slips back into his slouch. There are things I want to ask, impressions dying for a few details. I keep quiet.

I'm not the only one telling stories on my own terms.

·······•••••••·······

For supper the Hydes take me to a local restaurant called Thai Me Kangaroo Down. In the early part of the night, the conversation is harmless. "What's the latest back home? How is the Great White North surviving without you?" I pass on a few news items, things I have a vague awareness of since arriving in Oz: 2015 was the world's hottest ever year, but it was only the eleventh-hottest in Canadian history. The cover art of Drake's upcoming album, *Views*, couldn't be any worse than his previous one, *If You're Reading This It's Too Late*, which looks like it was done by a chimpanzee on a dare. True to my prediction at the start of the season, the Canucks have no chance to make the NHL playoffs.

"It's so different over there, isn't it?" says Nina. "I mean, for a country that's got a lot in common with us, there's a heap of things that make it, I don't know, foreign. Exotic, even." She scoops rice into her bowl and returns the dish to the center of the table. "There's something I wanted to ask you, Munro…if it's okay."

"Go ahead."

"Why here? Why an exchange to Australia? Was there something that made you want to come? Or some*one*?"

I set my chopsticks aside and wipe my mouth with a napkin. Possible answers to her query wheel through my mind. The trip as a poor substitute for Evie's aspirations? Nonstarter. A need to escape home for a while? Makes my parents sound like assholes—definitely not the case. A throwaway line about Down Under being a prime destination for every Canadian? It was Evie's dream, not mine.

There is one other option, something of a last resort. I suspect it will shut down any similar questions in future. I look around the restaurant. Too bad it has to be said in public.

Maybe you should tell the Hydes everything this time.

Maybe you should leave me the fuck alone for five minutes.

33

"Evie had this teacher. Mr. Adams. From Australia— Brisbane actually. She loved being in his class. She learned a lot with him, so many things that would've helped her live a full and happy life. She was thankful for everything he did. And, on the day my sister died, so was I."

A small gasp escapes Nina's mouth. Geordie has begun to perspire. A grim-looking Rowan asks a passing waiter for a refill of water. I fill my lungs, empty them.

"Evie and Mr. Adams were walking toward the library. Coming out of English class, Evie had said she wasn't feeling great, so Mr. Adams was holding her hand. He noticed the blue color of her lips was darker than usual. As they passed by the World War II honor board, Evie stumbled. Mister Adams said, *Oopsie doodles* and kept his grip, preventing a crash into the wall. He was about to suggest a visit to First Aid when Evie stumbled again. Second time was different. She was real heavy, as if invisible hands were pushing her to the ground. She dropped, and the weight was too much for him."

A group of fifteen or so at the large table in the center of the restaurant starts singing "Happy Birthday." The Hydes aren't distracted, all three leaning slightly forward in their seats. Nina is teary, her eyes and the tip of her nose shaded red. Geordie mops his brow.

Rowan has his arms folded tight, as if the temperature in the room has dropped several degrees. My throat is tight, but it doesn't stop the stream of words.

"Evie hit a drinking fountain with her shoulder, twisted and ended up on her right side. The group of students walking behind her—twelfth-graders—almost tripped over her. Mr. Adams told them to stand back and got down on his knees. He turned Evie over. She looked like she was napping. She looked like she was dreaming."

Wow, you know so much about what happened, Munro! It's like you were looking over Mr. Adams's shoulder!

Shut up.

"Mr. Adams worked on her for ten minutes. Chest compressions, occasional breaths. He didn't stop, not when the crowd gathered, not when the shouting and the crying started, not when one of the school captains fainted. He didn't stop when the first-aid officer arrived with a defibrillator. He kept going. He kept going when it was obvious he should give up. He still had his hands interlocked, ready for compression, when the paramedics took her away in the ambulance."

I cough once, a raspy hack into the crook of my elbow. The story's done. The stream of words is dry. Over at the birthday table they've broken out the sparklers.

"Mr. Adams," I conclude. "He's the reason I wanted to come here."

LIAR! LIAR! LIAR! LIAR! LIAR! LIAR! LIAR! LIAR! LIAR! LIAR! LIAR! LIAR! LIAR!

Amid the hand wringing and the tissue clutching, both Nina and Rowan zero in on Geordie. If he's aware of their attention, he doesn't let on. He pulls on the collar of his dress shirt and splits the silence.

"He did his best, Mr. Adams. That's all you can do. I hope he understands that." He presses on his forehead for a few seconds, then releases a breath, the sound like a hand pump inflating a bike tire. "Do you want to track him down, Munro? Is that what you're hoping to do?"

I shake my head. "I'm not here to find Mr. Adams, sir, but I do want to find his spirit. I think I've found some of it already in this family."

The flattery acts like a reboot. As per the first-day barbecue, the Hydes are immediately ready to resume the exchange they signed up for. Nina "goes for repairs" in the washroom and on the way back high-fives the birthday boy at the center table. Geordie teaches me a few verses of "Waltzing Matilda," assuring me the jolly swagman wasn't at all jolly but a very poor decision-maker. Rowan recounts the school day, rating my performance a nine out of ten, the loss of a mark due to my ill-advised wish for some Frank's Red Hot sauce to put on my Oz burger. By the time dessert is done and the bill is paid, the Hyde computer is back to normal, the Maddux blue screen of death now gone.

··········●●··········

Mom and Dad:

You'll be pleased to know I survived week one at Sussex State High. It's not as different as I'd hoped. I guess school is school, no matter what part of the world you're in. It was an okay week though. I will go back again next week.

I met the counselor (guidance, not crisis). She gave me the lowdown on everything. They're big on volunteering here—you have to do fifty hours in first semester of grade eleven. Not sure where I'll go at this stage.

Rowan invited me to do one of those escape-room puzzles with his friends next weekend. He says the place has an old Brisbane asylum setup for one of the rooms. You and Dad are probably hoping I don't get out. I don't blame you.

How's the foundation's campaign shaping up? Did the film shoot go okay? I'll keep an eye out for it on the website.

Ciao for now.
M

·········●·········

Ringing. A FaceTime call. It's six in the morning, Vancouver time. Perennial morning person Lou is on the other end.

"Yo, Munrovia! Awesome to see you, bud! How's the land of Silverchair?"

A pang of homesickness hits. Ah, Louis Erasmus and his stacks of retro grunge vinyls, all those tracks laid down before we were born. When I told him I was doing the exchange, he quoted one of the songs in his collection, something about me looking California and him feeling Minnesota. He held a hand to his chest as he said it. Much like he is doing now.

"Friendly," I reply. "They like the accent."

"Maybe they're mistaking you for Ryan Gosling."

"For sure. He's got the same chicken legs and pony-tail as me."

We gab for ten minutes, me doing most of the gabbing. I update him on the weather (hot), the Hydes (cool), the first week of school (I survived).

"How are the beautiful Aussie honeys?" asks Lou.

An image of Caro sneaks into my head. More a silhouette than an image. Nighttime. *Nuit.*

"I've only been here seven days."

"That's plenty long enough for Ryan Gosling." Lou presses forward. His Clearasil-ed face is huge on my phone display. "Come to think of it, I imagine you're the honey over there. You're the honey, and those Aussie girls are a bunch of bears sniffing around you."

"You got quite the imagination, Lou."

"Man, I wish I could get a bear sniffing around me."

"Thanks for the visual."

Lou smiles. "It's real good to see you joking around, homes. Been a while."

"True dat."

Lou starts flicking a pen around his thumb. He looks away. "So I'm sorry to kill the buzz…I saw your mom and dad at Save-On Foods yesterday. They told me you'd made it over okay, said you were settling in with your host family. They looked pretty bummed about the whole thing, to tell you the truth."

I rub my face and nod. "Yeah, the exchange was kind of a last resort to keep me in school. They only agreed because I thought it could work."

"I think they regret letting you do it."

"Yeah, I wouldn't be surprised. I'm making the effort to keep in touch though. I'm sending emails. And we'll FaceTime soon." I flex my hand, trying to shake off the pins and needles. "It's only six months."

"Six months," repeats Lou. He rakes his hair, turning his ginger bed of coals into a bonfire. "You sure you're coming back?"

"They don't do extensions, bud."

"No, I mean *you sure you're coming back*?"

My head drops. "Is this about what happened in the gym storeroom again? I told you fifty times already, Lou—that was a joke!"

"Dude, you picked up a starter's gun while Mr. Hofer wasn't looking. Then you pointed it at your chest and said you'd like to put a hole in your heart, same as Evie."

"I didn't say it was a good joke."

Lou pushes forward, crowding the screen. His grave face could double as a Halloween mask. "If you ever need to talk, I'm here for you, brother. Any hour of the day or night. Okay?"

"Okay."

"Okay?"

"Okay!" It's my turn to lean in. "So I need to talk now—about the Canucks. Or are you not finished going all Teen Helpline on my ass?"

You weren't joking when you put that gun to your chest, Munro.

Yes I was.

No you weren't.

It was a starter's gun. It didn't even have any caps in it.

But you thought about a real gun, didn't you? You thought about how it would feel in your hand. You thought about how hard you would have to squeeze the trigger. You thought about how the bullet would feel going into your body, how much pain there would be. You thought about how it would be over in a second. You thought it might not be the worst thing that could happen. I saw all that. In your head.

In your heart.

THE ESCAPE ROOM

The Nike douchebag is right in my face. From the nose up, he's blank. The whites of his eyes are dull. The pupils are pinholes. His blond bowl-cut hair is oily and limp. Below the nose, he's fuming. Mouth twisted, teeth gritted. The huge, angry zit on his chin is begging for a mirror and a squeeze. His breath is a disgrace.

"Fuck off, you skinny, ponytailed dipshit," he growls. "It wasn't a foul."

"What do you call this then, asshole?" I lift my forearm up to eye level. A big red welt runs from my watchband to my elbow.

Nike D-Bag's lips peel away from his crooked teeth. "You don't like playing hard? Then fuck off back to Iglooland and your figure-skating lessons."

I hold his stoner gaze. The murmurs of the surrounding spectators go up a notch. I can't make out what they're saying.

The talk in my head, though, is loud and clear.

He has no idea who he's dealing with.

I flex my right hand. Fingers scream. The back of my neck feels like it's about to split in two. I didn't go looking for a fight today. After waking up late and not being able to do my usual anti-Coyote exercises, I thought half an hour of pickup would be a decent substitute. I thought it would take the edge off.

A brawl on the basketball court—perfect way to finish week two. By my super-low standards, the first week at Sussex was a triumph. No meltdowns. No flashbacks. The Coyote was vocal but not totally intrusive. As the new outsider at school, I got a ton of stares and questions. I handled them all without puking pea soup or turning my head 360 degrees. It was a good, positive start. Entering week two, I was cautiously optimistic about the direction in which I was pointed. Who knew—maybe I could even get my hands on a compass.

I did not get my hands on a compass. I grabbed hold of a grenade. The pin came out Monday lunchtime with the girl lying on the grass next to the soccer pitch. She was flat on her back, one leg bent, one arm flung sideways. Friends stood around her, heads bowed. A dude with the collar turned up on his sports-uniform shirt was on his knees by her hip. One of the girl's sneakers had come off; it was upside down on the painted sideline, lime-green laces untied, a few feet from the friend circle. The reality of the situation, I found out later, was pretty tame. The girl had tripped running backward and smacked her head on the ground. A few circling stars, a few *there, there*'s. Nothing serious.

Trickles of sweat poured down my back. Armies of goose bumps marched on my skin. My lungs tightened. My head throbbed. My heart may have even stopped for a few seconds, cruel prankster that it is. I told the gang I needed to sit down in the shade, that the heat was getting to me.

More problems piled on after the girl on the grass. On Tuesday I had a panic attack during the school fire drill and ended up in the first-aid room, hyperventilating into a paper bag. On Thursday I froze during a practice book talk in English. And now, here it is, the icing on top of my week-two relapse cake. Friday-morning recess and some bowl-cut, swoosh-festooned fuckwad of a trog mauls me on a drive to the hoop, all but destroying my arm. And when I call him out on it, he decides he wants to throw down.

My heart is a wrecking ball, swinging away in my chest. Ollie's words itch like a mosquito bite: *You are not your thoughts.*

She's right! You are your actions!

Punch this asshole's lights out!

Nike D-Bag rolls a glob of spit around in his mouth and horks it onto the ground right next to my sneaker.

"What are you waiting for, dipshit?" he says. "You wanna go? Let's fuckin' go."

Though my right hand hurts like a mother, I ball it into a fist and draw back.

YES!

"NO!"

My cranked hook stalls. Somebody's holding it back.

"Let's go? Sounds like good advice, Mun."

Rowan. I wrestle with his bear hug, trying to lash out.

"You don't want to take on this one, Trey," he says to Nike D-Bag. "Ice hockey player. Knows how to throw 'em."

He hangs on to me and gets some help from Digger. The two of them muscle me out of reach.

NO!

The girls emerge from the onlooking crowd and add their two cents.

"Seriously, you got nothing better to do, Trey?" asks Maeve.

"Like shave your palms?" suggests Renee.

Caro confronts Nike D-Bag, feet apart, hands on hips. "Get in Munro's face again, Trey," she says, "and I'll let Mr. Wilson know you shoplifted your nice LeBron shoes there."

He laughs nervously, tells her to piss off and calls out to me. "Lucky your babysitters were here, dipshit!" He gives me the finger, accepts a bounce pass from one of his gangsta goons and shoots an air ball.

Rowan and Digger shunt me through the crowd and off the court. The girls follow. I'm released only after I've promised to be good. I breathe, counting down from twenty.

"No doubt Trey Jensen was outta line," says Rowan, wiping the sweat from his brow. "But that fuckwit outweighs you by fifteen kilo, brother."

"Twenty," corrects Digger.

"You got some kind of death wish, Munro?" asks Renee.

I stretch the fingers of my right hand. "Life wish, actually." I quickly add, "I've faced up to worse than him."

Caro begins examining the welt on my arm. It's a welcome development. And not unfamiliar. Caro went all Florence Nightingale on me after Monday's girl-on-the-grass flashback. Lots of *ooh*s and *aww*s and other sympathetic noises. The suggestion of a cold washcloth to put on my neck and forehead. And, best of all, she touched me. Four times. Twice on the upper arm, once on the shoulder and once on the face. It was a better treatment than the breath counting, the muscle releasing, the morning exercises, the *work with your unreasonable thoughts* mantra…all the Ollie-advised calming techniques put together.

"Thanks for having my back out there," I say. "All of you."

"No worries," replies Rowan. He consults with Nurse Caro. "Is he going to be okay for the escape room tonight?" She nods. "Good. Well, Munster, I think you've met your quota of trouble this week."

The others agree. Digger's phone bursts to life, looping the Darth Vader music from *Star Wars*. He checks the incoming text.

"From Kenny," he says. "Ms. Mac's done the placements for volunteering."

·············●·············

Fair Go Community Village is always looking for Living Partners to help make a difference and create meaningful connections with our special-needs residents.

You will provide friendship, coaching, education and experience to positively impact the residents' ongoing life journey.

You'll be a key part of the daily routine, with activities in the areas of vocational and educational training, community access, fitness and recreation, home maintenance and a multitude of other life skills and fun experiences.

The role of Living Partner is a wonderful opportunity for you as a young person with energy and compassion. You are the sort of individual who views time spent with our special-needs residents as a privilege.

No experience necessary.

We look forward to meeting you!

Rowan slides the printout back across the desk. He keeps his eyes fixed on our Biology teacher, Mr. Pearce, standing at the whiteboard like a six-and-a-half-foot, sweaty-armpitted, praying mantis. He murmurs through a cupped hand, "This your placement?"

"Yeah," I whisper.

"And you don't want to go here?"

"No!"

"Did Trey Jensen's devil breath melt your brain at recess? This joint seems like a pretty sweet setup."

"Not for me."

"Not for you? Ah, I see. Too much baggage—is that it?"

I flinch. My vision buffers for a second, stuck in its download.

You remember when you helped out on Evie's field trips? You weren't much help, were you? Wherever they went—Science World, the PNE, Watermania. Whatever the activity—eating lunch, crossing the road, walking in a crowd. You were always a helicopter. How is she doing? Is she enjoying herself? Is she listening? Is she learning?

You didn't have to watch out for her the whole time. You know that. You loved being there. Evie loved that you were there. That should've been enough.

But you couldn't help yourself.

Rowan looks down at the desk, begins tracing the scratches on the surface with his finger.

"I get it. Dad couldn't swim for a whole year after the rescue. We'd go to Coolum—his favorite place in the world to bodysurf—and he'd just sit on the sand, reading *Rugby League Week*. Sometimes he'd get the shakes and have to go back to the hotel room. Wouldn't even look at the water." He stops tracing. "It was hard." Several classmates turn and stare, their looks all communicating the same thing: *Shut your piehole.* Out front, Mr. Mantis scans the rows of bugs, looking for a lunch date.

I take two deep breaths. "This isn't the same. I just want to do my hours somewhere else. In a place that's... not a privilege."

Rowan adjusts his neck chain and shrugs. "If you say so, man."

"Can I change?"

"Doubt it. We call it the 'voluntold program' for a reason—you do your fifty hours where they say you will."

"Shit."

"Maybe Ms. Mac can help. Go see her after this."

"Rowan Hyde. Disturbing the peace, as usual." Mr. Pearce rubs his hands together. His voice suggests he's caught a fly. "A question for you, young man: a population or groups of populations whose members can interbreed and produce fertile offspring—what's the biological term?"

Rowan twists his mouth. "Can you repeat that, sir? My Canadian friend here may not have understood."

I shrink in my seat. Our classmates no longer want Rowan to shut his piehole. Mr. Pearce rolls his eyes, flicks his bony arms, presses his hands together. "Population or groups of populations, members can interbreed, fertile offspring produced. What's it called?"

Rowan slaps his desk. "Splendour in the Grass music festival, sir."

The room unloads. Mr. Pearce sighs and waits it out—the eye wipes, the fist bumps, the simulated sex acts. He grasps a red marker in his twig fingers and begins stalking the whiteboard. Rowan waits for his name to get written up, then leans over.

"Brother, if you want to avoid voluntolding at Fair Go, you're gonna need a pretty good excuse."

··········●··········

"You need a pretty good excuse," says Ms. MacGillivray, typing at speed of light, eyes fixed on the monitor. She has two long scratches on her neck. They look like a fish-gills tattoo I saw on Reddit. "Have you got a pretty good excuse, Munro?"

You do—you're afraid of this Fair Go place.

Tell her.

"I just thought students might, you know, have a choice. Seeing as it's a volunteer program."

Ms. Mac stops typing and gives me a sappy look. "Oh, that's a lovely thought. But I guess you haven't heard the students calling it the 'voluntold program.'" She stifles a laugh. "I wish we could call it that, honestly."

"So…I'm stuck."

"No, you're in prime position." Ms. Mac gets out of her seat and sits on the edge of her desk, hands in her lap. "You're away from home, on your own. Trying to fit in. And you've had a rough go this week, no risk. Yes, I heard about the fire drill Tuesday. And the spat on the basketball court at recess." She holds up a hand. "That's a conversation for another time. What I want to say right now is give this a chance, Munro. You told me in our first meeting that you want to be better. Fair Go is tailor-made for that. I hand-picked it just for you. Spend some time out there, and you will be better. I guarantee it."

I exit the guidance officer's digs wondering what a Bail Her Swift guarantee is worth.

......••••••●•••••••••

School week is done, eh? You made it.

No thanks to you.

So where are we going now? Where is this train headed? Sea World? Lone Pine Koala Sanctuary?

No.

Are we going to the beach?

I—not we—I am going into the city to a place called Liber8 with my new friends.

What is Liber8?

It's a bunch of rooms you have to escape from. They have clues and stuff. You race against the clock.

I think that's stupid.

What you think doesn't matter.

Yes it does. You brought me here to Australia. You wanted to "find a place for me to go." So, I want to go to the beach.

You will go to the fucking beach when I say so. Okay? I've got six months here, you know.

Not if you keep losing it.

"You're looking intense, brother," says Rowan, voice raised over the noise of the train. "Still mulling over that arsehole Jensen getting in your face on the basketball court?"

I quit leaning against the handhold by the doors and put my weight on both feet.

"I'm thinking about Fair Go, actually."

"Still?" Rowan pulls on the cuffs of his leather jacket. "Stuff it, Mun! That's in the future—this is now! Friday! You're coming into town for a sick puzzle-room breakout with your new mates. We'll go to the Snag Stand or Little Saigon afterward. Hungry Jack's in the mall, if we're really desperate. You look sharp, by the way."

Jeans, retro Grizzlies ballcap, old sneakers—apart from my Robbie Vergara tee, hardly sharp. I did take the elastic band out of my hair, so now I look sixteen instead of fourteen.

"You're in Australia!" continues Rowan. "Here for a good time, not a long time, so that's what we're gonna do." He digs into the inner pocket of his jacket. He pulls out a small plastic bottle with all the flourish of a busking magician. "I reckon this might help you loosen up."

"Coke?"

"Bundy and Coke." Rowan looks around for spying eyes.

"Bundy?"

"Bundaberg rum. Have some."

I bite my bottom lip. Booze: essential for mental-health recovery. In the summer after the funeral, I got wasted twice on "borrowed" Pabst Blue Ribbon, figuring I'd test out that whole drink-to-forget thing. Although it tasted like ass, the beer numbed the ache for a few hours. And it did sort of muffle the Coyote—it sounded like it was talking through a tin can. But I didn't forget, not for a minute. Not when I took a piss in my goalie mask or when I cried on Louis's shoulder or when I staggered into our front yard and threw up on the garden hose.

"Think I'll pass."

"You sure?"

"Yeah."

"Good time, not a long time?"

"I'm okay."

Rowan shrugs, glugs and stashes the bottle back in his jacket.

The train slows and comes to a stop. The stretch of Brisbane River we're perched over is flat, not a ripple in sight. It looks more like earth than water. Rowan taps me on the shoulder.

"This bridge—people live in it." He points toward the large concrete support to the left of our car. A line of windows runs up the center of the pylon. A small balcony at the top has a sad-looking plant and a line of laundry. "In 2011 pretty much everybody east of here went under."

Rowan digs up a short YouTube video called *Brisbane River Flood—Walter Taylor Bridge*. It shows the rushing river, brown and swollen and sweeping beneath the deck. Debris enters the shot: a pontoon dragging branches, a small white boat still attached to its buoy. I watch it twice, then hand the phone back.

"Pays to live up high, hey?" he says. "No rescue required."

A flush appears in Rowan's cheeks and ears. I don't know if it's the Bundy and Coke or the YouTube footage, but I have an inkling he's set to fill in a few blanks about his dad's heroic deed. Then the train lurches forward, pitching us both out of the moment. Rowan shudders and settles back into Friday-night anticipation.

"Caro is excited for this, brother. You were all she could talk about in Physics this afternoon. She even got roused on by Ms. DiMambro for being too chatty. That never happens with Caro."

"Glad I'm getting other people in trouble and not just myself."

"Yeah, well, I don't think she'll mind too much if there's, ahem, a bit of 'trouble' tonight." He does air quotes around the word *trouble*.

"Really? You went there?"

"Oh, I went there. What's the matter? Worried you won't get any alone time?"

"That's exactly what I'm worried about."

Rowan watches me fan the fingers of my right hand, then massage the palm. Before he can repeat his *good time, not a long time* spiel, I point to his jacket.

"Think I might try some of that Bundy and Coke after all."

·········●●●·········

Rowan and I meet the others outside Liber8. Digger is pumped.

"Been looking forward to this for a loooong time!"

"Didn't you do this two weekends ago?" asks Renee.

"Yeah. With my cousin."

"And *last* weekend?"

"Yeah. With my mum."

"So when you say you've been looking forward to this for a *loooong time*, you actually mean seven days."

Digger bows his head. "It was hard, I'm not gonna lie."

"Just make sure you don't give anything away," warns Maeve.

"Yeah, we'll tell Jessica Mauboy if you do," adds Rowan. "I doubt she'll want to come to a semiformal with a walking spoiler alert."

Digger swears under threat of electroshock therapy that he hasn't done the asylum escape.

We enter the foyer—it's a cross between a dentist's office and a nightclub—and Caro pulls me aside. Released from the buzz-killing Sussex school uniform, she is formidable. Mascara, eyeliner, deep-purple lipstick, dark-gray bangles. Hair like a black portrait frame. A bright-yellow dress contrasts the shadows. She's not breathtaking—she's breath*giving*. She's mouth-to-mouth resuscitation.

"Are you okay, Munro?" she asks, leaning in close to my ear to combat the shouting promo coming out of the giant monitor on the foyer wall. "I'm still thinking about how woozy you were on Monday."

The hand she has on my sleeve is burning a hole in my shirt. "I'm good. Just one of those things. Won't happen again."

"I brought a washcloth in my bag, just in case."

"That's very sweet of you, Caro."

She notices goose bumps on my arm and smiles. "Now you're cold! Mind you, so am I. The air con in here is cranked."

We pay our money. A listless guy with stretched earlobes appears from a back room and gives us blindfolds. Renee asks if she can have a whip as well. Rowan makes a crack about "fifty shades of Renee." I put my blindfold on; immediately my head feels heavy, as if the Grizz hat I'm wearing has been replaced by a football helmet. Lobe Guy tells us to line up single file and put our hands on the shoulders of the person in front. I clamp my left hand onto Renee. Caro— behind and at the end of the line—holds on to me, giving small squeezes.

Right there and then I think, This is good—this can all work out fine.

Evie would be scared if she was here.

She hated the dark. You know that.

And now she's in a box, buried in the ground.

When Lobe Guy tells us to take the blindfolds off, Caro, Rowan and I are in a cell with gray bars and white padded walls. Splotches of "blood" dot the floor under our feet. *HELP ME* has been scratched into one of the padded panels to our right. In the corridor outside the cell, there are three objects: a broom handle, a single work boot and a mounted picture frame with columns of weird symbols and numbers. A black combination lock secures the door. The air smells like bleach and sweat. Next door, I hear Maeve, Renee and Digger, laughing and whooping, the sounds leaking through a gap between the wall and the ceiling. From what I can make out, they're in a similar cell, same lock. Rowan surveys the space— barely big enough to fit three people—then pulls out the Bundy and Coke for a swig. He hands it over, and I do the same. When I offer it to Caro, Rowan intercepts.

"Not a good idea," he says, reclaiming the bottle.

"I don't drink," says Caro. She gives me a thin smile and twists one of the bangles on her wrist.

"Oh, I'm…I'm sorry, Caro. I don't like to drink either…normally. I mean, I drank a couple of times, over the summer, but it didn't do anything for me. So…yeah."

Lobe Guy comes to my rescue, asking for quiet so he can give us the background to our escape scenario. Standing in the corridor where we can all see him through the bars, he pulls a grubby laminated card from his pocket and reads aloud in the voice of the teacher in *Ferris Bueller's Day Off*. We are trapped in a "home for wayward girls" in 1920s Brisbane. One of our friends, Vera, has recently died after a prank gone wrong. She was in the attic, rope around her neck, faking suicide in the hope of guilting the headmistress out of her stern rules and cruel punishments. When the headmistress discovered Vera, she didn't notice the hidden chair she was standing on and lunged for her. The chair was knocked out from under Vera's feet, hanging her for real. Inconsolable over what she'd done, the headmistress flung herself out of the attic window, splatting on the ground far below.

Now we are locked up, accused of killing the headmistress as payback for Vera's death. We have one hour to escape the home, prove our innocence, avoid lethal injection and elude a vengeful ghost. Lobe Guy puts the card back in his pocket and stifles a yawn. If we need a clue to help us along, he concludes, we're to press the button on the remote provided. Rowan claps his hands as Lobe Guy locks the doors and departs. The digital clock high up on the dividing wall begins to count down.

"Let's GTFO."

These peeps are fun. A bit like your friends back at DSS, eh? I mean, the friends you used to have back at DSS. They didn't hang out with you much in the summer after Evie died, or when school started again. Apart from Louis. But even then, there were times he blew you off too.

I can't blame them, Munro. Who wants to be around someone sad and angry all the time?

That's not fun.

·········●·········

We're out of the cells and on to stage two.

I'm not really sure how that happened.

I remember Lobe Guy came and gave us a clue because we hadn't done squat in the first half hour. Then, after he left, Rowan and Caro figured something out that made Renee angry. She groaned and said, "Why the fuck didn't you notice that before? We're in this together!" It had to do with the stray boot on the floor, out of reach. And the broom. That was important. I'm not sure why. I wasn't paying close attention.

I tried, early on. I tried hard to think about the clues, what they might mean. I read out the number sequences on the wall so Rowan could work the lock. I listened to the others, speaking through the gap above our cells. I even suggested there might be something in the boot at one point. But as the number on the clock got smaller, and the noise of the gang increased, thinking became too much of an effort. I massaged my temples. I bit my nails. My groin felt like water. I sat out. Literally. I sat on the cell bench, trying to remember that this was supposed to be fun, that I was here for a good time. I shouldn't have had that Bundy and Coke.

I'm standing now in the second room, the others bouncing around me like Ping-Pong balls. The scene is grim. There's a handprint on the wall and more blood on the floor. A nasty-looking machine with wires and electrodes and switches with large handles is off to one side. A suicide note is taped to a large mirror beside the locked door; it's signed *Vera*. The ceiling lights are in metal cages. They flicker every now and then, as if spelling out a warning. In my hand is a disc, smaller than a puck, with lines that look like sound waves on one side. The digital clock in the corner shows we've just over twelve minutes left.

My legs are turning to jelly. There aren't any benches or chairs in this ugly room. I wish I was back in the padded cell.

At home, everyone knew why you were angry and sad. Apart from Rowan, these guys have no clue. They figure it's tough for a new kid coming from the other side of the world. But is it so tough that you're freaked out by a girl lying on the grass? Or you're in the face of some goof on the basketball court? Or you're afraid of volunteering with disabled people?

And now you're standing around like you're waiting for a bus while they work their butts off to get you out of this place?

The gang's voices are bleeding into each other, but I can still make out some of the talk.

"We need to get this open!"

"We tried that already!"

"It's gonna be something really simple!"

"Calm down. Let's think it through."

"Look at the time!"

I'd like Caro to stand behind me again, put her hands on my shoulders. That would feel good. That would help.

I lean against the wall. The bricks are cool on my cheek.

Six minutes left.

Not a long time. But enough for a good time?

Let's have some fun, Munro.

Weird smoke is gathering around my feet. The walls creak and groan. Someone screams. I flinch, look around. The gang is still going about its frantic business.

Didn't they hear that?

No, they can't hear it. Only you can hear it.

And see it.

You have four minutes.

There's a body on the floor. On its side. Tucked in next to the machine with the wires and the electrodes.

It's the suicide girl from the story, Vera. She'll have a clue for me. She'll get me out of here.

It's Vera.

I know it's Vera.

You know it's not Vera.

You have three minutes.

She's not dead.

She's dying.

She needs to be turned over, put flat on her back. She needs compressions.

I look at the others, hoping they can help. They're busy. They've found something. A box. *The* box. Opening it gets you out of here.

Where's the key?

Two minutes left! Time is running out!

It's up to you!

Every second counts!

I kneel down beside the body. Before I can turn her over, I need to get rid of this disc in my hand.

On the other side of the room, one of the gang shouts. I think it's Renee.

"Munro! He's got the key!"

Under a minute!

Get to work, Munro!

My hand.

It's in agony, but I can't open it. It's locked.

"Munro! You've got the key! Give it to me, mate! Before it's too late!"

Twenty seconds!

SAVE ME!

"MUNRO, GIVE ME THE KEY!"

TEN SECONDS!

SAVE ME, MUNRO!

"LET IT GO, MUNRO!"

SAVE ME!

"LET GO!"

"JUST LEAVE ME…THE FUCK…ALONE!"

A loud buzzer sounds. The lights—flickering and dim before—turn up to full brightness.

I blink. The floor is bare. Vera is gone. My right hand slowly opens and spreads. The disc falls to the floor. There's an imprint of its wavelike lines in my palm. I press it against my aching chest and stand, surveying the scene. Renee is a few feet away, pale, breathing hard, fingers probing the point of her shoulder. Hair is thrown across her face, as if a gust of wind caught her unaware. Maeve stands to the left of Renee, biting her lip. Digger stands to the right, covering his O mouth. The two of them look like deer in the headlights. Rowan, arms folded, is holding the box we failed to unlock and leaning against the door we failed to open.

Caro.

Her bright features are blurred at the edges. She's got questions. Concerns.

Lobe Guy appears, seemingly out of thin air. He wanders into the middle of our silent movie and plants his hands on his hips. He has a toothpick in the corner of his lopsided grin.

"Whaddaya reckon?" he asks. "Did ya have fun or what?"

........●..........

Louis goes offscreen for a few seconds. When he reappears, he scratches at his nest of red hair. "So let me get this straight. The clock's counting down to zero, and this Renee, she grabs your hand, trying to get the 'key' you're holding, and you yell at her. And as you're yelling, you...shove her?"

I shake my head. "I pulled my hand away from."

"But she got hurt, right?"

"I kind of yanked her shoulder."

"You pulled pretty hard then, Mun."

"I guess. It was just a reflex."

"A reflex?"

"Yeah. You know, like when somebody taps on your knee with a little hammer."

"Uh-huh." Louis sucks air through his teeth. "What happened after your reflex?"

"Nothing much. I said sorry, asked if she was okay. She said she was fine. She apologized for grabbing my hand. She said she got too caught up in the moment. We all went to Snag Stand after that to get something to eat. It was awkward. No one wanted to do much or talk much. So we just went home."

Lou sighs and leans to one side. "James lost his shit completely when we did the Egyptian room in Richmond. Those escapes, dude. They can bring out the worst in people."

Or they can just show people as they really are.

"Something went glitchy in there, didn't it?" asks Lou. "Did you have, like, a flashback or something?"

"No."

"You sure?"

"Yeah, I'm sure!" I hold my hand against my ear and press the buttons on a pretend phone. "Hello, Teen Helpline? Yes, I'd like to speak to Louis Erasmus, please? What's that? He's too busy being a jerkface?"

"Quit it, bro. I know you had episodes and stuff at home."

"This isn't home."

"What happened there, what you've just been talking about…sure sounds like home to me."

Smart boy, that Louis. Very smart boy.

Lou leans in to the camera. "Don't be mad at me, bro. How about we switch gears, eh? What was that place you said you were going to be volunteering at? The residence for disabled people?"

"Fair Go."

"That'll be pretty rewarding, I reckon."

"Oh, God."

"What?"

"You sound just like the guidance counselor at Sussex. You going to guarantee Fair Go will make me better too?"

"I think it'll stop you yanking the shoulders of those Aussie honeys." Lou throws his hands up. "Ah, crap. you're still mad." He makes his own pretend phone and puts it down on the table in front of him. "Lookit, the jerkface is hanging up. He's off shift. He's gonna call up a sex hotline instead."

I laugh. "I'm hanging up for real."

"I'm here for you, Munro."

"Worst sex hotline ever."

"I'm here for you. Don't forget it."

Lou starts licking his lips and rubbing his nipples. I flip him off and kill the call.

·········●··········

The role of Living Partner is a wonderful opportunity for you as a young person with energy and compassion. You are the sort of individual who views time spent with with our special-needs residents as a privilege…

We look forward to meeting you!

I switch off the lamp and turn onto my side. In the darkness, my left arm splays sideways, holding the printout off the edge of my bed. Sometime between awake and asleep, the paper slips out of my fingers and falls to the floor.

·········●··········

A wonderful opportunity, it says. It will help you get better, they say. You know what I say? A place like that will make you worse.

Is that even possible after what happened this week? The fire drill and the freeze-up in English class? The near-fight with the Nike D-Bag? What I did to Renee in the escape room?

Of course it's possible. Anything could happen at Fair Go. So many reminders. So many bad associations.

Someone could collapse there. Someone could die. Fair Go could be the last straw, Munro. One visit—just one—could mean the end. Of school. Of the exchange.

Of you?

..........●..........

Evie? Are you there? I don't know what to do, Evie. Tell me what to do. Talk to me.

Why can't you answer? Why are you the only one that's off limits? I'm supposed to hear you. I read that it happens a lot. I read that it helps the people left behind to cope. But you haven't spoken to me. Not once. Why? Do I have to die too? Is that the deal? I have to die before I can hear your voice again? That hardly seems fair.

I looked after you, Evie. I taught you stuff. I protected you. You know how a clown fish takes care of the coral reef it lives in and vice versa? You were my coral reef. You were my world. You were my bud.

All I hear now is the fucking Coyote. I can't stand it, for everything it's done and everything it's doing. The day it goes away will be the greatest day of my life.

I hate it.

I don't hate you, Munro. I'm here for you.

Unlike Evie.

AN INTERVIEW

Wow, Munro! It's Sunday, and you're on the train. You'll be at Fair Go in ten minutes! Why the change of heart, amigo?

Lou and Ms. Mac felt I should give it a go. They think it could be good for me. I trust them more than I trust you, Coyote.

More than you trust yourself, you mean.

Whatever.

They'll be very proud of you.

I'm sure.

I'm very proud of you.

Fuck off.

Fifty hours though…that's a long time to be in a bad

place. Maybe you should quit now, before things, you know...end.

Fuck. Off.

Don't swear! I'm trying to help you.

I'm not listening to you.

···········●···········

The interviewer enters the office. I stand and button my jacket.

"Sorry I'm late," he says, extending a hand. "Table-tennis match went into extra time...I lost. Couldn't find the table with my last lob. I'm Kelvin Yow, residential manager of Fair Go."

"Munro Maddux."

"Take a seat, Munro."

"Thank you."

"So. You're from Vancouver, Canada?"

"Yes, sir."

"Love the tie."

"Thank you, sir."

I pinch the knot under my chin. The fabric is printed with squirrels in sunglasses throwing up the horns. It was Evie's last birthday gift to me. She wanted me to wear it to grad.

"Call me Kelvin," he says, lifting a small tube of candy labeled *Fruit Tingles* from a drawer in his desk. He tears the silver wrapping and pops a piece in his mouth. "You're on an exchange?"

"Yes, sir...Kelvin."

"Sir Kelvin—I like that. You've been here...what, two and a bit weeks?"

"That's right."

"How you finding the heat?"

"Not too bad."

"Good-o. And how's the new school?"

"Up and down."

"Oh. Bit of an adjustment period, I imagine."

"Something like that."

For the first time since sitting, Kelvin Yow registers as more than just the guy in charge of my potential last straw. His face shines, like he uses wax instead of face wash. He wears a wolf's-head ring on his right index finger. I look around his office. No motivational clichés or roller-derby merch here. A *Star Wars* poster has pride of place on the main wall, only the writing is in a different language, maybe Italian: *Il ritorno dello Jedi*. A *Walking Dead* coffee cup stands guard beside his open laptop. Framed photos are everywhere; each one features two people in the shot. Kelvin is the constant, smiling, arm over the shoulder of his companion. The others? I'm guessing they're the residents.

"Let's get to it," he says, levering a second Fruit Tingle out of the tube with his thumbnail. "Do you have any experience with the disabled?"

It flashes through my mind to say no, but I don't want to feed the Coyote, not this early in the proceedings. I sit up straighter in my chair. Shrug. "I grew up in a special-needs home—my little sister had Down syndrome."

"Had?"

"She died last March. Heart failure."

"Ah, geez." Kelvin brings his hands together under his chin and closes his eyes. He murmurs words I don't recognize, maybe a Buddhist prayer or something. "I'm really sorry for your loss, Munro."

I assume my brutal, superficial honesty will force Kelvin to drop the subject. He doesn't.

"That's hard on a big brother, no doubt."

"Um, yeah. It is."

"Especially if it's sudden."

"Yeah."

"Was it sudden?"

"It was…yeah."

He shakes his head. "That link between Down's and heart issues…"

If there's a second half to the sentence, it's jammed in his throat. He resumes eye contact, and for a brief moment I see the same expression Mom and Dad have exhibited for close to a year: unwavering acceptance.

"You okay, Munro?"

I blink, swallow. Aside from a tense grip on the chair's armrest, I find I am okay.

"I apologize if I upset you."

I loosen my tie. "It's okay."

Kelvin puffs his cheeks. "Not sure about that. How about I stick to the script for this next bit?" He pushes his chair back and stands. "Let's head across to the Rec Refuge."

..............●............

When I first arrived, Fair Go took me by surprise. It was bigger than I thought it would be. A couple of buildings and a bunch of cabins—that's what I'd expected. A souped-up version of summer camp. Now, accompanying Kelvin through the heart of the community, I realize the full scale of the place. It's a tiny town. A tiny hometown, in fact. Several of the sights are like snippets of my hood back home. The vegetable gardens and the barn and the field stretching toward the horizon could belong to Westham Island. The arts-and-crafts store wouldn't look out of place in Ladner Village, next to Stir Coffee House or Angela's Boutique. The small skateboard space next to the library is a mini-version of the park by Delta Gymnastics Society.

There's also plenty that tells me I'm a long way from home. Palm trees. Patches of dry grass out of sprinkler range. The Aussie flag fluttering above the admin building. Metal roofs on the townhouses. Laundry on a rotary clothesline. The signs on the swimming pool fence: *NO SHARKS IN THE WATER* and *BEWARE OF ATTACK TURTLE*. The overall vibe of Fair Go, though, is familiarity. Comfort. I recall the Coyote's warning from last night: *so many reminders.* My hateful sidekick got that much right. So far, none of the nasty variety.

I suspect the residents like living here.

Where would you have lived, Evie? After grade twelve, would you have stayed home with Mom and Dad? Would you have gone out on your own? Maybe someplace in between? Somewhere like here?

I often wonder where you are now. And who you are. Maybe you have superpowers. Can you run like the wind, or fly, or turn invisible? I hope you're still you though. Two legs. Two arms. Brown hair. Blue eyes. 'Celebrity' chromosome 21, as Mom and Dad used to say.

Mom and Dad believe you're in Heaven, Evie. I'm not so sure there is such a place. Right now, I still believe in Hell more than I believe in Heaven.

Kelvin gives me the Fair Go facts as we walk.

"The residence was the brainchild of my father, James Yow. He was the youngest of four children. His eldest brother, Wally, was diagnosed as 'mentally retarded' at the age of five. After his schooling was finished at seventeen, he was placed in an institution. Dad loved Wally very much, and he always felt sad that his brother had to move away. He didn't blame his parents—Grandpa died of polio before Wally was in his teens, and Grandma kept Wally at home until her own health concerns made it impossible to continue without serious help. Responsibility, Dad felt, lay more with society. He decided he would do something about it. So he built a place for young disabled people coming out of school, one that struck a balance between independence and support."

We pass by an obstacle course—*WOOT CAMP*, according to the hand-painted sign, the *B* crossed out and replaced with a *W*—threading through a crowd of thick trees. In the center is a spiderweb of ropes suspended between two poles. Half a dozen people have a girl held high on their hands and are attempting to crowd-surf her through the top gap in the web. For a second I think she's scared, curled up and shouting louder than a substitute teacher in detention. Then I put two and two together—the wheelchair off to the side, her jerky movement. She's not shrinking in fear; she has cerebral palsy. And she's having a blast. On cue, she raises her bent arms and starts singing Imagine Dragons' "Radioactive" in a loud, tone-deaf voice.

"Fast-forward a decade, and here we are," says Kelvin, continuing the speech he's probably given a thousand times. "Fair Go Community Village, the place where special needs and life purpose come together. Fair Go sits on seven acres of land; there are twenty residents living in the fully furnished, fully appointed townhouses. There is a staff of twelve full-time and twenty-eight part-time staff employed here. A number of the full-timers, including me, live in the dedicated staff units on site. We offer a range of vocational opportunities: small-scale agriculture, creative arts, recycling, hospitality, basic digital media skills. Fair Go makes pesto and jams and chutneys from our homegrown fruits and veggies. We sell them in our shop, and in a few stores around West Brisbane. Arts and crafts are also sold in our shop, as well as on Etsy. All the info can be found on our website, which is in large part maintained by two of our residents." Kelvin pauses midstride. "I should also mention that we encourage peer-to-peer training. Good example over there."

He points toward the parking lot. A small team of damp, energetic car washers are sudsing up a "ute"— a vehicle, I've discovered in my short time here, that can't decide if it's a car or a truck. The leader is a big guy in board shorts and a T-shirt with some sort of dinosaur or sea-serpent print. His head is turned, like he's looking elsewhere, not really paying attention. His voice says otherwise. His instructions are clear: dip deep into the water, don't squeeze, wash with a clockwise motion, separate bucket for tires, thick sponge for the rims, thin sponge for the windows, chamois after rinse. He says "no lie" a bunch of times.

"That's Perry Richter," says Kelvin. "He was going to be a resident here at one point, but his family circumstances changed and he didn't end up making the move. So now he shares his car-washing expertise with the residents. He also does a bit of basic first aid."

Kelvin waves. Perry responds with what appears to be a kung-fu kick. We walk on.

"Personally, I think Living Partner is the best role in Fair Go. It's what really separates this place from any other care facility around. Each LP has five residents assigned—they are your crew. The task is quite simple: be there. To listen, to talk, to play, to guide. Develop rapport, build a relationship. Hang out. Become someone the Fair Goers look forward to seeing and spending time with. It's a life-changing experience for a young person, no doubt about it."

Kelvin leads me into a gymnasium-type building that has a climbing wall in the first room, and bikes, treadmills and weight machines in the second. We make our way up a winding ramp and stop outside a door that says *Rec Room* 1.

"Any questions?"

I shrug. "When do you make your decision?"

Kelvin grins and opens the door. "I don't decide, Munro. These guys do."

Five residents are seated behind a long table in the center of the room. Kelvin ushers me over.

"Righto, some quick intros before the formalities. Munro Maddux, this is Bernie, Shah, Blake, Iggy and Florence."

I offer my hand to each. Two of the five accept. Shah nods and yawns; Iggy offers a bent elbow instead of a hand; Florence leaves me hangin.' I sit in the chair in front of the table.

"This is your interview panel, Munro. Each of the residents has a question or two prepared for you. Answer them as best you can. Now, I realize we have a language difference here—you speak English, and we speak Australian. If there are any hassles, I'll interpret. At the end of the questions, the panel will vote using a ballot to determine whether you get to do your volunteer hours here. All five panelists must vote yes for you to be our next Living Partner."

"Do you vote as well?" I ask.

Kelvin smiles and plants himself on a stool off to the side, next to an air-hockey table. "You're here because I already voted yes. If I thought otherwise, I would've said goodbye to you back at my office. Okay, we good to kick off? Bernie?"

Bernie stands, clears her throat, slips her hands into the pockets of her cargo shorts. For a few seconds she blinks rapid fire, as if there's a strobe light behind her eyes. Her hunched back gives her the appearance of a bass clef. She begins pacing back and forth in the space between me and the table.

"When I was eleven, my family went to Wilson's Lookout to see Riverfire. Before the fireworks started, I wasn't paying attention properly and I stood on a blanket that belonged to the lady next to us. She got really angry and said I was rude and had no manners. She said I got that from my parents."

"Bernie," says Kelvin.

"My mum told her that I was special needs and I didn't properly understand social situations or personal space."

"Bernie—"

"The lady then called me the R-word. She said being an R-word was no excuse."

"Bernie!" Kelvin forms a time-out T with his hand. "Munro's only here in Australia for six months, so you need to hurry up with your question, hey."

Bernie stops pacing and puts her hands on her hips. She moves in front of me, dips her head and stares at my tie.

"Do you use the R-word?"

I lean forward to catch her gaze. "Never."

I have a story to share too, about a boy, Vincent Perrault, who lived on our street. He called Evie a "dumbass retard" twice. Third time, I chased him down, pinned him, arm-barred him back to his house. I told his mom what he'd done and said the next slur would see me beat the living snot out of her "precious little Vinny." He never trashed Evie again—never said anything at all to us, in fact—and the Perraults moved to Calgary the following year. I'm ready to launch into this story, but Bernie seems satisfied with my one-word answer. She applauds and returns to her seat. The strobe light behind her eyes is out.

"Shah, you're up," says Kelvin. "What's your question for Munro?"

Shah yawns again. "You here for good?" he asks.

I hesitate, then answer. "I'm on a high-school student exchange. From Vancouver, Canada."

"You leave family behind?"

"Yes."

"You here alone."

"I have an Australian family, the Hydes, I'm living with for the next six months. And I'm getting to know the people at school."

"But you here by yourself. You are alone."

"Yeah, I am."

Kelvin holds up a hand. "Okay, Shah, that's good enough, hey?"

Without answering, Shah rises, turns his chair around and sits facing the opposite way. A chunk of skull about the size of a golf ball is missing from the back of his head. What look like burn scars are poking out of his shirt collar.

Kelvin scratches his cheek and sighs. "Righto, let's move on, shall we? Blake, you're next."

I shift in my seat. Blake. Brown hair. Blue eyes. She has the Down's features—flat face, pixie ears, big tongue. She's similar to Evie with one glaring exception: she's an age my sister will never be.

I wait. If the Coyote is right about things getting worse, this is the moment to tell me all about it.

Still waiting.

"Do you have a girlfriend?"

"Still waiting."

Blake's giggles shake me loose. I glance over at Kelvin.

"Don't worry, my man," he says, winking. "You've only been here a couple of weeks."

"I'm sorry," I stammer. "I misheard the question. No, I don't have a girlfriend."

"Not in Canada?"

"No."

"Not in Australia?"

"Like Kelvin said, I've only been here two weeks."

"Is there someone you've met that you like?"

"I've met a bunch of people I like."

"No! I mean *like* like."

I rub my eyes. "There is a girl at school."

Blake makes a *woo* sound and tucks a strand of hair back over her ear. "What's her name?"

"Caroline. Caro, for short."

"Are you dating?"

"We're texting."

"Every day?"

"Most days."

"You think you might marry her?"

"Righto, that'll do for your 100 questions, Blake," says Kelvin. "This is Fair Go, not eHarmony."

"I've got a boyfriend. Dale in number 6," adds Blake. "He never gets jelly."

"Jelly…not sure that version of the word is on Dale's iPad. Okay, Iggy, over to you. The floor is yours."

Iggy makes a show of attempting to stand. Several groans later, he gives up.

"I am not feeling the best," he says. "My lungs. So I'm going to stay sitting. My question is, have you ever done CPR on anyone?"

A breath snags in my throat. My right hand clenches.

"Whoa, Ig," says Kelvin. "That might be a bit rough, mate. How about you ask something else."

"Why? A Living Partner has to know CPR, yes?"

"That's right, but—"

"So I want to know if he's good at it. Just in case he needs to do it on me."

"Iggy, it's way too harsh to—"

"I'll answer it," I say. My breathing has steadied. My hand, though clenched, feels no pain. I'm still here in the interview and not teetering on the edge of the world. My mind is clear.

Nothing, Coyote?

Kelvin's pinched face turns my way. "You sure you want to answer?"

I nod and fix my gaze on Iggy. "I, uh, didn't save the person. But it wasn't because my skills were bad. It was…It was…The person couldn't be helped at that time. CPR wasn't going to be enough."

The deep discomfort I ought to be suffering belongs instead to Iggy. He shrinks into his seat, melting like a January snowman in a March rain. I move to the table and go down on my haunches.

"You and I both hope you'll never need CPR. But if you do, and I'm here, I'll do it, and I'll do it well. You're in good hands. I'll even shake on it."

I kink my elbow and hold it over the table. All eyes—even Shah's—are on Iggy. His eyes are on me. The melt has stopped. His bent arm tentatively emerges from the blanket. We make brief contact and then he coughs into his shirt sleeve and squirrels his arm away again. I go back to my seat. Bernie bursts into a round of applause. Blake sticks two fingers in her mouth and whistles.

"Sweet!" says Kelvin. "Okay, Florence. I know the question you're going to ask."

Florence licks her lips. Her teeth are pretty messed up—three of the front four are missing, as well as a few more toward the back. Her nose is pushed to one side. She looks like she wants to do similar damage to my face.

"You ever hurt your sister?" she says.

"Florence!" Kelvin steps toward me. "Munro, wow, I'm so sorry. Flo usually asks people if they know how to defend themselves. I had no idea she was going to…"

The rest of Kelvin's apology fades. Florence's question is only that—a question. It should be a knife to the gut or a hellish scream or a car going off a cliff. But it's not. It's just...words. And I'm putting words together in reply. Coolly. Calmly. Without the Coyote to contend with. Did I ever hurt Evie emotionally? Sure. When I was six, I put her Jessie doll in the garbage disposal. When I was eleven, I told her she'd get diarrhea if she went on the Zipper at May Days. When I was fourteen, I showed her the sex scene in *The Fault in Our Stars*. Did I ever physically hurt my sister? Just one time. I broke her ribs pressing on her chest, trying to save her life. I can give all these answers if I want to, even the last one. But I won't. I have a different response.

"I don't have a sister."

Florence scrunches her nose. "Too bad," she says. "I would teach her Flo-jitsu." She moves to the side of the table and performs a short physical sequence that looks like an angry robot trying to kick a soccer ball. "My own martial art."

Kelvin fans his face with his hand. "Okaaaay. Well, that was...educational. If no one has anything more to add, I'll get the ballot box and the papers." He collects a notepad, pens and an empty Streets Blue Ribbon Neapolitan ice-cream tub from a cupboard in the corner of the room. Placing them on the table, he lays out the rules. "*Yes* or *No* on the piece of paper, no names, fold it once, drop it through the slot in the top of the tub. And don't try to sneak a peek at anyone else's vote."

Blake and Bernie are the first to cast their votes. Blake blows me a kiss. Bernie gives me a sneaky raised thumb. I think I'm cool with them. Iggy has brought his blanket up over his head and is completely obscured as he marks his slip. A small pale hand emerges and scrabbles around for the tub, eventually finding it with some "getting warmer, getting warmer, really hot…got it!" assistance from Bernie. Then it whips back under the blanket.

Two left—the two major question marks.

Shah sits poised over the paper. He watches me as the pen descends and starts to scribble. There's the flicker of a smile as he drops his vote through the slot.

Last one.

Florence gives me the stinkeye and pretends to karate-chop her pencil. She deposits her paper in the tub, then sits back in her chair, arms folded. If she could get her hands on a microphone right now, she would drop it.

"Done!" announces Kelvin. "I'll take the box. Munro, we'll go back to my office and find out if Fair Go is in your future. Bernie, Shah, Blake, Iggy, Florence, thank you for your time. We'll see you at dinner, and I'll let you know the result then. Munro, after you."

As we depart Rec Room 1, I hear Blake say in a loud voice, "You two better not have fucked this up for us!"

The warning is met with a solid belly laugh.

..........•..........

"Gotta say," says Kelvin, lowering himself into his office chair and putting the *Walking Dead* coffee cup to one side, "there were a couple of interesting moments there. You handled them well though."

"Yeah, that was a…surprise."

"Not put off, are ya?"

"Not yet."

"The rest of your six months in Oz will be a breeze after that." Kelvin shakes the ice-cream tub and peels off the lid. "Righto, ready for the count?"

He plucks them out one by one and lays them open on the table:

One—*Yes*. With a smiley-face.

Two—*Yes*. With the *e* backward.

Three—*Yes*. And a *please*.

Four—*YES!!!*

I edge forward in my seat. Despite fears and doubts, I decided to give Fair Go a shot. And what's happened? Nothing. A big, beautiful, silent nothing. Screw the sample size of ninety minutes. I'm calling it: this place will not make things worse. But can it live up to Lou and Ms. Mac's hype? Could it actually make things better? Something was definitely happening in that interview. Something promising, hopeful. Something that makes me want to come back.

Kelvin extracts the fifth ballot, opens it, holds it where only he can view it. He glances at me, then back at the slip of paper. An age passes. The office contracts. The zombie on the *Walking Dead* cup tries to bait me into a staring contest. At last Kelvin bites his bottom lip and shakes his head. He lays down the final vote.

Yes.

No *please*. No exclamation marks.

Just *Yes*.

The residential manager extends a hand across his desk. "Congrats, Munro. You can call yourself a Living Partner now."

I meet his firm grip. "I think I will."

Kelvin escorts me to the front entrance of Fair Go. The Brisbane sun is low in the sky, its rays now moving through my body rather than beating me over the head. The grass in and around the Welcome sign is brown and thirsty. A smell like cinnamon is in the air. A throng of dark clouds hangs out by the horizon.

"Know your way back to the station?" asks Kelvin.

"I do. It's pretty straightforward."

He looks at his watch. "You've got about ten minutes, so you're sweet."

"Great, thanks."

Kelvin claps me on the shoulder, goes to turn away, pauses. "Hey, I'm sorry again about that question from Florence. I don't know why she asked that…well, I *do* know why she asked it, but I don't know why she asked *you*."

I look at the Welcome sign. I didn't notice the *o* had a smiley-face when I came in.

"I can honestly say it didn't bother me," I reply.

"I'm glad." Kelvin flicks a thumb over his shoulder. "Every resident lives with adversity, Munro. Some, like Florence, live with too much."

"Is she still living with it?"

He pulls a weed from the dry grass and wipes his hands. "Not physically. Her brother went to prison for what he did to her. And Flo's a tough bugger. They all are."

Kelvin departs with a wave that's almost a salute and heads back into the Fair Go grounds.

·········●·········

On the train, thoughts fly by as quickly as the scenery. What did happen in that interview? Where was the Coyote? Is this a breakthrough? If it is, will it travel beyond the boundaries of Fair Go Community Village? As an immediate test of my newfound resilience, I pull out the novel we're doing for English, *Picnic at Hanging Rock*. It's supposed to have hot private-school girls and murder and be creepy as hell—all good stuff. I open it to dog-eared page eighteen and begin shoveling the snowbank of words. By page twenty, I'm hoping a plow comes by. Barely any of it registers. I guess I'm not cured.

Reading has been this way for longer than I can remember now. Ollie assured me difficulties concentrating and staying on task were temporary. Things would improve with time and space and kindness to self.

But how long is temporary?

Where were you?

Ah, Coyote. Welcome back. I missed you so much.

Where WERE you?

You know where. I was interviewing for my volunteer hours.

Why wasn't I there?

Maybe you can't go there.

Are you trying to trick me?

No.

You can't trick me, Munro. I'm too clever for that. You can do morning push-ups and count your breaths and think good thoughts and all the other things Ollie told you to do. You can pretend you don't see me or you can't hear me. You can bring me to Australia, hoping I'll stay. It doesn't change anything.

We'll see.

No, YOU'LL see. You can't just walk away from me, Munro! If you think I'll just say goodbye without putting up a fight, you need to think again!

Okay, you can stop now. You've made your point.

You know you can't let go of me. You did it with Evie, and you know how that turned out.

Fuck.

The one time she needed you to hold on, and you couldn't do it.

I am Munro Maddux. I am a good person. I am not responsible for what happened.

You could do it every other time. But when she needed you most? When her heart stopped?

I am Munro Maddux! I am a good person! I am not responsible for what happened!

You couldn't do it—that's why she's dead.

I AM MUNRO MADDUX! I AM A GOOD PERSON! I AM NOT RESPONSIBLE FOR WHAT HAPPENED!

You're the reason she's dead.

IAMMUNROMADDUXIAMAGOODPERSONIAMNOT RESPONSIBLEFORWHATHAPPENED!

That's why I'm with you, Munro. That's why I'm here.

I AM...MUNRO MADDUX...I AM...A GOOD PERSON...I AM NOT...RESPONSIBLE...

Forever.

I AM...MUNRO...MADDUX...I AM...NOT...GOOD...

I stumble out through the doors of the train as they close behind me. The platform sways and rocks, but I manage to stay upright. My heart booms like a cannon.

"Mun! Did you forget your stop?"

"Whaaa?"

"Whoa, dude, your backpack. It's caught in the door! HEY, HEY! OPEN THE DOORS!"

I turn my head. Rowan is jogging toward me. Gum in his mouth. Skateboard under his arm. Panic in his eyes.

"DON'T GO!"

It's okay, Rowan. It's over now. The Coyote backed off.

"HIS BAG! HE'S STUCK!"

My feet are dragging, but it's over now.

"STOP THE FUCKING TRAIN!"

There's a heave and a hiss and a sigh. I'm still. I fall forward, and Rowan catches me by the shoulders.

"Holy shit, Munro! You all right?"

"I'm okay. It's over now. No big deal."

"Did you know you were caught in the door?"

"It's over now. No big deal."

"Well, being pinned all the way to Central Station would've been a big deal." He drops the skateboard onto the concrete, starts rolling it back and forth under his sneaker. "I'm guessing things didn't go too great at Fair Go."

"I start next weekend."

"Oh. Okay. That's…awesome?"

"It might be."

"You sure you're okay? You look like someone ran over your dog."

"Coyote. That would be good."

"Hey?"

I wave a hand. "Forget it."

Rowan stops his skateboard roll. His eyes narrow. "Man, I know there's more to your story than you're willing to give up. And that's cool—it's totally your business; you can do whatever you want. But take it from someone whose family went through a real rough patch: find somewhere or someone to talk to. And soon. Before the next fight on the basketball court or the next Liber8 freak-out or the next train door that wants to rag-doll you to Roma Street."

I hook my thumbs under the shoulder straps of my bag. An image of Fair Go's Welcome sign flashes in my mind. The *o* has an upgrade to its smiley-face—a wink.

"Let's go," I reply.

·········●··········

The fast walk home helps shake off the lingering effects of the Coyote's attack. By the time I open the screen door at the Hydes' house, I'm feeling close to Munro Maddux levels of normal again.

"MUNSTER AND ME ARE HERE!"

Nina appears in the hallway, carrying a clear, bubbly drink in a tall glass. "You're back! We're just watching the cricket. How'd you do at Fair Go, Munro?"

"Good."

"Oh, I'm so pleased. I know you were worried about it."

"I got a thumbs-up from the residents, so I'm in."

"The residents?"

I tell her about the interview—the setup, the vote. I don't get into the questions asked or how I answered them without incident.

"Did you have to bribe any of 'em?" asks Rowan.

I shrug. "Just the manager."

"And what work will you be doing there?"

I explain the Living Partner role. Rowan makes impressed noises.

"Sweet gig, hey, Mum," he says, increasing the chewing rate on his gum. "I have to scrub toilets at Habitat for Humanity."

"The needy families who move into those homes—they'll appreciate those sparkling loos." Nina pats her son's shoulder, then sips her drink. "Munro, it's very admirable what you'll be doing at Fair Go. Fitting, too, because of…well, it's fitting…"

"Thanks."

"I think your sister would be very proud of you."

I remove my backpack, put it between my feet. "You're right, Nina. She would be proud."

"And as your other mother in Australia, I'm proud of you too."

"When do I get an other mother?" asks Rowan through a burst bubble.

"When you send your real mother round the bend… which will be a blessed relief for her."

"Cool."

Nina takes another sip. "Okay, Munro, I'll leave you be—unless you want to watch the cricket with us?" On cue, Geordie starts shouting and swearing at the TV, something about a ball down the leg side and the umpire's finger not doing what it was supposed to do.

"On second thought, maybe you'd rather not put up with a retired copper acting like he's still on the job."

"Yeah, I might pass, Nina. I've got some schoolwork to do for tomorrow."

Nina turns to her son. "Hear that, Rowan Hyde? Munro's going to do schoolwork." She exits, giving him the "I'm watching you" sign.

Rowan smirks and points at me. "I should've let you ride to Roma Street, brother."

...........●...........

Picnic at Hanging Rock gets another shot at kicking my ass. After half an hour, I tap out. I open up my laptop and go to the website I've been avoiding since my arrival in Australia.

The new video—the one Mom and Dad were working on when I left, the one I was afraid to be filmed in—is up on the Foundation's home page. I click *Play*, fold my arms and lean on my elbows. A series of photos featuring Evie drifts in and out of the frame, backed by a Sarah McLachlan tune. As the montage fades to black, my mother and father appear, standing in front of our house, holding hands. Mom begins: "Evelyn Maddux had a smile that would light up a room. She had a laugh that made you want to tell her a joke. She had a spirit that overcame every challenge that stood in her way. Evelyn Maddux was our daughter, and she was the very definition of life. Tragically, that life was far too short."

Dad's turn. "The eighth of March will mark the first anniversary of our beautiful daughter's passing. To remind us all to live the way Evie did, and to help fund research and awareness of Down syndrome, we ask you to buy this button."

A graphic of the button appears. The word *E-LIFE* is in bold yellow, set against a blue background.

"You can find these at Save-On Foods, Safeway, Best Buy and Canadian Tire stores, or you can purchase direct through the Evelyn Maddux Foundation. Thank you for your support."

The video fades with the two of them holding a button toward the camera. Just before they disappear, Dad gives his a kiss. A pop-up asks if I would like to see the video again.

"No thanks," I say aloud, exiting the screen and shutting the laptop. "I'm good."

THE STRAYA TOUR

Everything.

What?

Everything.

What's that supposed to mean?

It's like Jeopardy. *Clue: This hasn't changed for Munro Maddux in his student exchange so far...What is everything?*

Did it take you this whole train ride so far to come up with that? Golf clap for you, Coyote.

Hey, don't go wasting that bad attitude on a Sunday. Save it for school. After all, you need to top what you did in week three, eh? Another flashback—this one walking out of the library. Janitor found you crying near the

tennis courts. Another freeze-up in your English present-
ation. Not practice this time—for real. You were lucky the
teacher…what's her name?

Ms. Nielsen.

You were lucky Ms. Nielsen gave you an extra point
because she liked your accent. And then there was fight
number two.

It was just a bit of a scrum.

Fight, scrum…let's not split hairs. The main thing
is, you taught those three tenth-grade boys a lesson.
Douchebags. Who could possibly think surfing was better
than snowboarding? And then they're dumb enough to
say it out loud! Talk about asking for it!

Yeah.

The gang didn't have your back this time, did they?

Rowan did. And Caro.

Not the others though. On the basketball court, they
came to your defense. This time—not so much. They felt
you were being pretty douchey yourself.

I said sorry afterward.

How many sorrys is that now?

Fuck, why couldn't Fair Go be a couple of
stations closer?

Ah, you're still thinking Fair Go is some sort of safe
place. I've got news for you, Munro: it's not. First time

there, when I went missing—that was a mistake. I'll be right alongside you today. I'll be everywhere.

And everything.

·········●·········

Kelvin directs me to sit on the couch and plonks down beside me. He's gone casual; in our one previous meeting he was all business—dress pants and collared shirt. Today it's jeans, sneakers, sunglasses and a black ballcap with a masked-bandit logo. His T-shirt says *I Bring Nothing to the Table.* His office has a new look as well. A small bookshelf, stuffed full, sits under the *Il ritorno dello Jedi* poster.

"Ready to rumble?" asks Kelvin.

"Yes." I adjust my Canucks cap. "I was thinking if I could get hold of some equipment I'd teach them floor hockey."

Kelvin nods. "Sounds fantastic. Now forget all about that." He slaps his thighs. His face is lit up like a Catherine wheel. "Munro, my man, this is going to be a whole different caper to what you were expecting."

"What do you mean?"

He tells me. The team decided during the week that hanging around Fair Go for my stint was not going to cut it. Young man in eleventh grade, visiting from

Canada, never been to Australia before—he needs to see the sights! They came up with a plan. Every session until my fifty hours are up will be a stop on the Munro Maddux Australia Tour, or "Straya Tour," as they preferred to call it. We'll visit places in and around South East Queensland of the residents' choosing. Each resident will get a turn, in an ongoing rotation.

There is more.

Kelvin will come along as well. It means extra time put aside midweek for paperwork, but something like this is worth the sacrifice. He will be supervisor, bus driver, cash machine and videographer. When I ask about the last one, he explains that this is a chance to tell a great story—a group of residents showing off the city while getting recreational opportunities themselves. It is too good to pass up. As an afterthought, he asks if I have a problem with being in the video. I say I don't.

"So it's field trips the whole time?" I ask.

"That's what the team wants to do."

"A ton of sight-seeing."

"There's a lot they want to show you."

"And all five of them are good with it?"

"All five."

"Florence? And Shah?"

"So they say." Kelvin looks over the top of his sunglasses. "I'm sensing you're a bit uncomfortable with this."

I'm uncomfortable with being away from Fair Go. The Coyote threatened to be everywhere and be everything. So far, in my short time here, it's been nothing. For all I know, the physical environment is the reason why.

"This feels weird," I reply. "It's not really for residents. I mean, they've even given it a title using my name. I don't want them doing this for me."

Kelvin throws his hands up in mock disgust. "Man, it's all about you, isn't it? Typical bloody teenager!" He laughs. "Yes, you're the inspiration for why they want to do this. The catalyst, if you will. But like I said, there's plenty in this for them too. Believe me."

"I guess I had it in my head that I'd be helping the guys do stuff at Fair Go. You know, here, where they live."

Kelvin smiles. "Yes, they live here"—he jerks a thumb over his shoulder—"but they also live in the world out there." He stands, and I get to my feet too. He gives me a playful punch on the arm. "This is a unique opportunity, mate. So go with it, yeah? You never know—they might still become floor-hockey legends."

·········●●··········

There are five familiar faces on the bus. The sixth requires an intro.

"Dale is joining us on the 'Straya Tour," says Kelvin, talking over his shoulder from the driver's seat. "Functional interaction in the community is a big focus for him, so this fits the bill perfectly."

I wave. Dale waves back, then taps the iPad in his lap. An artificial voice responds.

G'day.

"Communication app," says Kelvin, inserting the key in the ignition. "Great stuff. Allows the user to have a voice, literally and figuratively."

"He's my boyfriend! Remember?" adds Blake, who is sitting beside Dale, head on his shoulder. "I told you about him at the interview! I said he doesn't get jelly!"

The iPad responds: **I like ice cream much better.**

I move down the short aisle, past Iggy—he's fogging up the window with his anxious breathing—and the seemingly unconscious Shah. Three from the back is frowning Florence. The seat beside her is free. Without acknowledging me, she shifts to the middle, taking up both seats, in case I had any ideas. I sit across the aisle. As I buckle up, Bernie rises, makes her way to the front of the bus and strikes up a conversation with Kelvin, who waves a hand and says, "Fine, fine. Don't take too long." Bernie takes hold of the bus's microphone, pulls her rounded shoulders back as far as they will go and clears something awful from her throat.

"Hello, everyone. Welcome to our first field trip on the Munro Maddux Straya Tour. Munro, I hope you're excited. I'm very excited. I know the others are too." She pauses. Shah's snoring fills the gap. "This is a great chance for us to show how awesome we are, not just to our brand-new Living Partner, but also to the people out there."

"You're pointing to the forest," says Blake.

Bernie shifts her aim to a more populous point on the compass. Blake approves. Kelvin fires up the bus.

"Can we go now, Bernie?" he asks.

"Soon." Bernie points. "Florence, what do you do if someone calls you the R-word today?"

"Drop-kick them in the throat."

"Uh…no. Don't you remember what we've been taught? S-N-A-P? SNAP? Blake, what does the S stand for?"

"Stop!"

"That's right! We tell them to stop. What about the N? What's that?"

"Now?" suggests Kelvin. "As in, 'Let's leave now'?"

"No, that's not correct. Dale?"

Dale types his response and holds the iPad up so it's better heard: **Name the behavior.**

"Yes! Call it out. 'That's rude,' or 'That's mean.' Now the A. Iggy?"

"Away?" says Iggy, blowing his nose. "Get away as quickly as you can."

"*A* is for *advise*. Advise them what will happen if they do it again. And, last, the *P*?"

"Please?" suggests Kelvin. "*Please* let's leave now?"

"No, that's not correct. Munro, do you wanna guess?"

I look to Florence across the aisle, who is poking at her teeth. "Punch them in the throat?"

"*Prove* it! Do what you said you would do! Whether it's telling someone or refusing to walk away or taking a photo of them to put on Instagram later. Stop, name, advise, prove. *S-N-A-P*—SNAP!" Bernie's speed-blinking paces her march up and down the aisle. She closes her hand into a fist. "Everyone say it together. SNAP! SNAP! SNAP! SNAP! SNAP! SNAP! SNAP! SN—"

Bernie trips on a stray bag in the aisle, stumbles forward and drives her still-extended fist into sleeping Shah's stomach. He jackknifes and lets out a yowl, then a torrent of angry words in another language—presumably swearwords—before stomping to the back of the bus. Awkwardness rules for a few seconds, and then laughter erupts. Blake roars like a bear. Dale is full of snorts. For good measure, he types *LOL* on the iPad and hits some sort of repeater button. Iggy giggles into the crook of his elbow. Even Florence cracks a half smile. Bernie waits for the commotion to die down, then apologizes for her behavior. She sheepishly airs one last "Snap" and takes her seat.

Kelvin swings the bus toward the exit.

··········•··········

In the online stuff I've read about trauma treatment and recovery, one message always stands out: when you find something that works, keep doing it.

Something worked when I visited Fair Go and met the residents for the first time. And I want to keep doing it. One problem: I haven't figured out what the something is. I don't even know where to look.

My team is probably a good place to start.

Iggy is staring out the back window of the bus at the trailing traffic. Every so often he points and ducks down in his seat. Florence watches his behavior. To my surprise, she does so without a scowl or a frown or an eye roll.

"We bein' followed again, Ig?" she asks.

He nods. "Green Camry. Rusty bonnet. Front left headlight is smashed in."

"Orright."

"It's been on our tail since we got on the highway."

"Well, it is the highway, mate. Hard gettin' off until there's an exit, hey?"

Iggy's unconvinced. He shakes a finger at the window. "Clever to be a couple of cars back and not be right behind. But not clever enough."

"How 'bout we play the name game?" Florence starts tagging cars as they pass by. Commodore, Falcon, Astra, Fiesta. Iggy is reluctant to join in—someone has to keep an eye on the green Camry—but then gives over. Pajero, Tarago, Jazz, Tundra. He mentions there's a North American vehicle called the Dodge Avenger. Florence sniggers.

"Does the Hulk drive one?" she asks.

Iggy doesn't answer. Instead he demands a thumb-wrestle. Florence tells him he's a stupid bugger, that he's been owned every time they've battled in the past. Iggy is undaunted. He stays in the contest for a bit, twisting his wrist, using his whole arm for leverage, cheating. At one point he tells Florence to look at the Hulk driving a Dodge Avenger in the next lane. It doesn't work. Florence fake yawns and pins him, sparking yelps of pain, a tap out and an excuse of "not feeling one hundred percent."

When the whining subsides, conversation kicks in again. The topic? The self-defense class Florence is hoping to get going.

"I got some things sorted," she says. "We could do it in the Shed, or maybe the fitness room, if it's only a few people. I know the moves I wanna teach. The Roo

Punch, the Redback Bite, maybe the Noosa Rip. Stuff like that. At the end I'll give my students a special belt I'm makin' in the art studio. It's white, and it's gonna have jacaranda flowers on it. It'll be tops."

"I'd like to do that class," I say.

Florence looks my way. Her nostrils are flared. What teeth she has left are clenched.

"It's not for you."

"Why not?"

She looks me up and down. Her lip curls. "'Cause you have to be disabled. Or a girl."

"Do you do a class for boys?"

"Why would I do a class for boys?"

"Because everyone needs to learn self-defense."

Florence looks at Iggy. He nods and rubs his thumb. She turns back to me, looking down the crooked line of her nose.

"Thumb-wrestle," she says. "You win, you can be in my class."

"Um, okay."

I begin "warming up." Flexing, stretching. As a goalie, your hands have to be strong and quick. I figure I've got a shot here. Iggy feels the same, or at least suspects it will be a decent contest. He's hard up against his seatbelt, straining to get the best view possible. Florence cricks her neck.

"Ready?"

"As I'll ever be."

"Hold out your hand. No, not that one, the other one."

"My right?"

"Yeah. I always wrestle with my right. Hold it out."

I don't comply. I bite the inside of my cheek. My legs bounce.

"I'd like to stick with my left, if that's okay."

Florence rears back. "It's not okay! I always wrestle with my right! Put out your right!"

"I can't do that."

"Do it!"

"I'm sorry, Florence. I can't."

The self-defense teacher-in-waiting throws up her arms, then drives her elbow into the seat padding.

"I s'pose it's a draw then," says Iggy. "Does that mean Munro gets to do the class?"

"It's *not* a draw," cries Florence. "We didn't even go one round!"

"He didn't lose."

"I didn't win either," I say. "That was the deal to do the class." I lean forward, trying to catch Florence's huffy, turned-away face. "Another time, maybe? When my right hand is okay?"

"Whatever. I'll still crush you."

"I've got no doubt you will."

·········●·········

Bernie has selected today's tour stop—South Bank Parklands. "My favorite place in Brisbane, maybe even the world!" She beams. As we walk through a Triffids setup called the Arbour, she takes hold of my elbow.

"Indigenous people from two different tribes met here for many years. Then the whites came along and took over, setting up Brisbane's main businesses. But then the river flooded in 1893, and the businesses moved to the north side because the ground was higher. By the way, I should tell you—there were two other big floods here, in 1974 and—"

"In 2011," I say.

Bernie lifts her sunglasses and squints her eyes. "You know about that?"

"Bits and pieces."

She stares, perhaps trying to figure out which bits and pieces. After ten seconds or so she finishes her sentence. "In 2011, where we are now, the water would have been up to our waists. But they fixed the damage."

For half an hour, the team and Kelvin and I laze about on South Bank's artificial beach. Bernie's focus shifts from history to engineering. She delivers a stack of trivia: the amount of water, where the sand comes from, something about dredge pumps and sifting machines.

"It's actually called Streets Beach," she adds. "Streets is a company that makes ice cream. My favorite Streets ice cream is the Golden Gaytime."

"I wish they'd called it Golden Gaytime Beach," says Blake.

"I wish they had too," I reply.

Bernie's history class resumes over lunch at a place called Cosmos. "The World Expo was held here in 1988, and after it was over they didn't want to leave a big hole in the ground, like what happened in your home city. In Vancouver, they didn't have a plan for what would happen after the Expo 86. Did you go to the Expo 86?"

"I wasn't born then, Bernie."

She blinks several times, gives me a look that says, *What a lame excuse.* She continues. "Here, they got lots of ideas for what should be built after the Expo, and in the end the Parklands was the winner. A good thing— nothing beats this place."

Tour guide Bernie finally goes on break at the Nepal Peace Pagoda. Prompted by a girl wearing a

Game Grumps T-shirt, she tells me about the clothing line she's working on at Fair Go. "I want to make shirts that say something I like, that have a good message."

"You got any ideas?"

"I thought about *SNAP*. But there's heaps of that on clothes already. I don't think it has the same meaning as our SNAP."

I'm about to suggest *R-Word* crossed out in a red circle when a small boy wearing his chocolate snack as a beard appears between us.

"Your back has a big hump like a camel! Does it have water in it?"

Bernie immediately responds, "*S* is for *STOP!*" and shoots out her hand. The boy thinks for a few seconds, picks his nose and smiles.

"*G* is for *GO!*"

He shouts and jump-slaps a high five. Before Bernie can progress to *N* (a name for this behavior doesn't instantly spring to mind), the boy's mom arrives on the scene, gasping apologies and threatening to take something called "Dorothy the dinosaur" away when they get home. They scurry away. Bernie watches the retreat, then pushes her sunglasses farther up her nose.

"I think I will make hats as well as shirts."

Quality time for Iggy and me happens two hundred feet up, looking out over the city.

"I like the Wheel of Brisbane," he says. It's the first time today I've heard him speak without a wheeze or a groan or a sniffle. "No one can follow you up here. And I think the chances of being killed are probably a lot less than on the ground."

"Okaaay. You're, uh, probably right."

"Do you like heights, Munro?"

"I don't mind them. I've been on the Sea to Sky Gondola back home. Peak 2 Peak up in Whistler."

"Has anyone died on those?"

"I don't think so."

"I'm not surprised."

As we arc toward the highest point, Iggy takes a sketchbook and a pencil out of his backpack.

"Drawing the city?" I ask.

"No. I'm drawing Infecto flying over the city."

"Infecto?"

"My superhero. He has the ability of germs, so he can go airborne. He can drink poison or get a virus in his blood or get a disease in his body, and he won't die. He won't even get sick. And when he's got the toxic stuff inside him, if he touches a bad guy, the bad guy gets really sick straight away and dies."

"Am I allowed to have a look?"

Iggy pulls the pad in close against his chest. "I don't let anyone see Infecto. I'm keeping him a secret until I've finished the story."

"No problem—that's totally cool. Would you mind then if I guessed what Infecto looks like? You don't have to tell me if I'm right or wrong. It'd just be for fun."

Iggy first looks left, then right. "Righto," he says warily.

"Awesome!" I clap my hands as the Wheel carries us over the top. "Okay, let's see, I guess if he flies, he'd have a cape, and I figure that cape would be made out of…sanitary wipes, maybe? Or prescriptions for antibiotics? Now the suit. It would have to be one of those hazmat deals, only skintight, and on the chest would be, like, the outbreak symbol or the skull and crossbones. Oh, I know! A petri dish with stuff growing in it!"

Iggy pushes his tongue into his cheek. He peeks at his drawing and snorts.

"Okay, last but not least—the mask. What sort of mask would Infecto wear? Gas mask, maybe? Probably not—that's more a villain thing. How about just the small plastic deal over the nose and mouth? You see people wearing those all the time in winter. Of course,

Infecto's mask would be a lot better than those—it would probably be made out of really thin gold or silver or platinum. Yeah, platinum. And for sure it would be really decorative with lots of different germs painted on it, you know? The way you'd see them under a microscope." The Wheel starts bringing us back down to earth. "That's all I got. Did I nail Infecto?"

Iggy wipes his eyes and *tut-tuts*. There is serious color in his face. He's grinning like he just saw Stan Lee.

"You said I don't have to tell if you're right or wrong."

"Correct."

"Then I'm not telling."

"Probably a good idea. Let's shake on it."

I lean and extend my elbow. Iggy meets me halfway.

·············●············

At the start of the day, Blake had me constantly double-taking. The briefest glimpse could convince me, just for a second, that Evie was here. The longer the day has gone on, though, the more I'm seeing differences rather than similarities. Dale being on hand is a big help. Evie never had a boyfriend (unless you count Chris Hemsworth), so the sight of this tall, skinny, silent sidekick wasn't ever going to hit home. And maybe his behavior—holding her bag, looping his arm through hers, the occasional butterfly kiss—emphasized the "Blake-ness" I'd previously been blind to. She has dimples. She flicks her hair a lot. She's quite light on her feet. Her lips are not in the least bit blue.

"You didn't answer my question," she says.

"Sorry, Blake?"

"The question I asked at your interview."

"You asked a lot of questions at the interview."

"You didn't answer the last one: are you going to marry your girlfriend, Caro?"

I take off my Canucks lid, pour some water in it from my bottle, jam it back on my head. "First off—she's not my girlfriend."

Not yet.

"Thanks for that, Dale."

No problem.

"Caro is very cool. I like her a lot."

"So she will be your girlfriend," says Blake.

"We'll see. "

"You want to make her your girlfriend."

"Maybe."

"When?"

"I don't know."

"Soon?"

I whisper in Dale's ear. He types.

I DON'T KNOW! shouts the iPad, volume to the max.

"Blake, if it happens, I promise you and Dale and the iPad will be first to know."

The clunk of bike gears and the clap of flip-flops fills the space in our conversation. Below us, a big paddle-boat churns the river, the white wake like a bandage on the water. A herd of people lean out over the rail of the Goodwill Bridge, waving and shouting and holding out their phones. Their reward is a horn blast.

"Do you want to marry *someone* one day?" asks Blake as the echoes die away.

I laugh and point at the markings on the pavement—a yellow bike and a 10 km/h speed-limit sign. "You're going way too fast here! Slow down, eh?"

She gives me a look that says, *What are you talking about? I'm walking!*

I shrug. "I'm sixteen, Blake. I'd like to live a little."

"So you *will* get married one day."

"If I've lived a little."

"And when you fall in love." Her head leans to the side, suddenly heavy. She takes hold of Dale's hand and swings it high, back and forth. "We can't get married."

"No?"

"We're not allowed."

"Oh."

"My dad said so. He thinks if we get married, we will want to live in the same house at Fair Go and sleep in the same bed and have sex and have children. He thinks we want to be the same as everyone else. Doesn't he?"

Dale allows a grunt to speak for him instead of the iPad.

"Do you want that?" I ask.

Blake halts the hand swinging. "We don't want to be like everyone else. We just want to get married. That way we'll be together forever."

·········●·········

If Shah was supposed to be anything more than a passenger on the trip, he never got the memo. Or he got the memo, tore it up and burned it. For the entire time at South Bank he was distant, hands in pockets, uttering a grand total of maybe ten words. His only real moment of life? A Champions League match on the big TVs at the Piazza.

On the bus back to Fair Go, I park myself in the seat beside him.

"Hey, I'm really looking forward to your turn on this tour business, Shah. You want to give me a hint where you're going to take us? Maybe a soccer game in the—"

"Football."

"Sorry?"

"Not soccer. Football."

"Ah, right. Of course. In Canada, football is a different—"

"I would like to sleep, thank you."

"You want to sleep?"

"Yes. I do not want talking now. I want to sleep, thank you."

"Okay. Sure, no probs."

Shah cozies up to the window. He makes a fist and presses it to his mouth. It kind of looks like he's sucking his thumb. Then he closes his eyes. I don't know when or even if he goes to sleep, but he doesn't move. Through the wail of an ambulance siren, through the jolts of speed humps, through an impromptu sing-along of Adele's "Someone Like You" initiated by Bernie, he is a corpse.

I squirm in my seat. A part of me wants to wake him. **Come on, Shah! We haven't spent any time together! With the others—even Florence—I took a step forward. We made progress. I listened and hung out and began building relationships. If I'm to keep the Coyote at bay, I need you too, bud!**

The silver lining? I'm talking to myself, and it's still just me.

I've taken zero photos to mark my first Fair Go adventure, and here at my shoulder is a beauty. I can see the image on Instagram and its accompanying caption: *One of my team, Shah, demonstrating the effect of chillin' with yours truly #Sleeper #TheSleepening #YouSnoozeILose #NoSleepTillBrisbane #FairGo #LivingPartner.* I leave the phone in my pocket though. This moment can be put away in the place that suddenly seems inviting.

My memory.

·········●●●·········

Kelvin gives me a fist bump. "Congrats, Munro. You did great for your first stint as a Living Partner."

"Thanks. Best time I've had so far in the exchange."

"Awesome. I take it you're feeling a bit better now about this tour caper?"

"I am. The Fair Go vibe travels."

"It does. Recorded some beaut footage today, by the way. You and the crew keepin' it real. Top stuff."

I nod, although I'm surprised. I don't recall seeing Kelvin with the camera in hand at any point during the day. Either he was very sneaky or I was very comfortable. Probably a combination of the two.

"It was a good start with the team," I say. "Florence, she's tolerating me. Shah though. I'm still at the starting line with him."

Kelvin shrugs. "Don't take the sleeping thing personally. He does it on all our community-access trips. He's got a pretty good reason."

Sounds specific. Maybe chronic fatigue syndrome, like Mr. Twan at DSS? That thing where you have sleeping fits—what's it called? Narcolepsy? Or maybe he has heart issues. Evie often fell asleep after school.

"Is it something I should know about?" I ask, trying not to be too nosy.

"No, it's fine." Kelvin finds a spare Fruit Tingle in his chest pocket. "He'll tell you if he wants to." He tucks the candy between teeth and cheek so he can keep talking. "You've got plenty of time."

••••••••••••••••

You were gone again.

I was. Are you going to put another smackdown on me?

Is that what you want?

No.

Do you want to be punished?

No.

You deserve to be punished.

No, I don't. I deserve to be better. And it's starting to happen, Coyote. Fair Go is making it happen.

You're just hiding, Munro. Do you remember what you did after the ambulance took Evie away? You stumbled around the school, past rooms and through doors. Along the side of the theater, around the tennis courts. Didn't stop until you reached the storage shed. You went in and you sat between the lawn mower and the spare recycling bins, and then you lay down on the concrete. And you stayed there so that all those people who wanted to say how sorry they were, and how it wasn't your fault, and that you did your best, and you should go home… you stayed there so they couldn't find you.

You hid, Munro. And now you're doing it again. You think this is hide-and-seek and Fair Go is where you can't be found. But I will find you. And when I do, you'll know we're together.

Forever.

I jerk awake.

Bright lights above. Hard cushion beneath. *Clackety-clack* in the ears. Runaway backdrop in the window. The PA announcement. My station—Wattle Ridge—is next.

I exit, jumping well clear before the door clamps shut and the train glides away from the platform.

....•.....

Maeve, Digger and Renee haven't had a lot of time for me since Liber8. But Rowan isn't deterred. He still wants all of us to get along. According to him, we just need an outing with a little less intensity.

"How about we go to the movies? See the new *Star Wars*? That'll be fun, hey, Munster?"

"I don't think so."

"Come on, man. Caro would deck me if I didn't bring you."

"Is Renee going to be there?"

"Mate, don't worry about Renee. We all love her, but she can be a pain in the arse at times. She knows that. She shouldn't have grabbed you at Liber8."

I appreciate his honesty. To fully show my appreciation, I decide to make an appearance. I'm feeling good. Solid. The connections with my team today, the absence of any bad moments on the tour, my assertiveness with the Coyote on the train home...the Fair Go effect is a thing. I had my fingers crossed it could travel; now I'm wondering how far it can go.

At the theater, it's clear things are a bit icy. Maeve and Digger bring me into the chat, but more out of politeness than genuine inclusion. Renee says nothing to me directly other than "How's it going?" I nod and smile. For Rowan's and Caro's sakes, I won't make waves.

If my presence is awkward for Renee, it doesn't register. During the pre-movie ads, she gives a standing ovation to a truck ad with talking bulls and then enlists Maeve's help in outright booing a tampon commercial that calls for women to "have a happy period." When the preview of *Batman v Superman: Dawn of Justice* hits the screen, she begins loudly suggesting an alternate title—*Fapman v Supergland: Dong of Justice.*

Caro leans toward me. "I know from past experience she can be more entertaining than the movie."

By *entertaining* she means "distracting." And I want a lid put on it before the words *In a galaxy far, far away* climb up the screen. *Star Wars*, I'm confident, will be plenty entertaining without Renee's look-at-me act.

Turns out she's on her best behavior and I'm distracted anyway. When Kylo Ren uses the Force to interrogate Poe Dameron, I wonder how he would fare against Infecto. As Rey smokes her attackers on Jakku, I imagine her receiving a Flo-jitsu belt as reward. Looking at the massive ditch surrounding the Starkiller Base, I figure they didn't learn anything from when they hosted Expo. My attention, of course, is also at the mercy of Caro. We share an armrest, and every time she shifts, my level of self-esteem is in direct proportion to the amount of elbow contact remaining. When Kylo Ren gets all murdery with Han Solo, Caro grabs me like it's a fire drill and my forearm is the personal possession she wants to take with her. She lets go soon after, but the mark left behind is a phaser strike. For the rest of the movie, I cling to the hope that another old-school character—Leia, Chewie, C-3PO, even Admiral Ackbar—will meet a shocking end. Sadly, they all survive.

"So where to now?" asks Maeve as we exit the theater.

"Across the road to Nitrogenie," says Digger. "I've got a hankering for one of those lemon, lime and bitters shakes."

"Yeah, I could go for a Pavlova Pash," admits Renee.

"Hell, I could give you one of those." Digger puckers up and advances, arms outstretched.

Renee shows him the hand. "I'd rather get one from Chewbacca."

Rowan looks my way. "How about you, Munster? Keen to join us?"

The corners of my mouth turn down. "I don't know. What's your plan, Caro? You sticking around?"

"Nah, I'm a bit tired. Don't like the look of that sky—reckon there'll be some thunder and lightning later tonight. Think I might bail. Want to share a cab home?"

"Sure. Is there a rank around here?"

"There's one just around the corner."

"Cool."

"You're taking Munro away?" says Maeve. "Who are we going to show the sights to now?"

"Yeah, we had a whole thing planned," adds Digger. "A river cruise, a dance at Cloudland, a trip up Mount Coot-tha."

Renee huffs. "You used to be such a party animal, Munro. We don't even know who you are anymore."

I pout and feign shedding a tear. Their sarcasm is uncalled for, but I don't give a shit. I'm feeling solid, and I'm heading home with a hot girl. And Rowan approves. He wanders over, eases between Caro and me, drapes his arms over our shoulders. "At least our Canuck friend here still likes *one* of us. Could well be some thunder and lightning this evening."

I glance at Caro. She's blushing, but she's not disagreeing.

••••••••••••••••••

We sit apart in the back of the taxi. In the space separating us, we each have a lone hand, palm down, flat on the seat. The gap between them can't be more than the width of a gum packet.

I blankly stare at our driver's turban, trying to come up with something to say.

You remember the last time Evie tried to ride a bike, Munro? At the old racetrack, beside the rec center? She told you she was going to stay up. She was going to ride all by herself. You told her to climb aboard, feet on the pedals, hips locked and not all loosey-goosey like they usually were. You said you would run alongside for a bit, then you'd let go so she could stay up. Ride all by herself.

Evie pushed on the pedals and the bike moved forward. You told her to keep pushing, keep going. You told her to keep it straight. As the bike picked up speed, she asked if you were going to let go. Soon, *you said. She asked you again. Just a little more speed,* you said. Evie's voice rose. Munro, let go! *But you kept holding the handlebars and the back of the seat. That's when she started to shout:*

LET GO!

LET GO!

LET GO!

"You have a girlfriend at home, Munro Maddux?"

I tap my forehead, clearing space for Caro's question. Rain patters on the roof of the taxi.

"Didn't you ask me that already? Two weeks ago in Chemistry class?"

"I remember. And now I'm asking you in the back of a taxi. You have a girlfriend back home, Munro Maddux?"

"No, I don't."

"Boyfriend?"

"Not that I know of."

Caro laughs. She pulls on her seat belt, creating some give that allows her to semiface me. "Ever wish you had a brother or sister?"

I'm thrown. Where did that come from? Then I recall—I told her I was an only child. First time we talked, first day of semester. I inwardly sigh. This night was going so well.

"I wish I had a sister," I reply.

"Yeah? Why so?"

"I just think being a big brother would be awesome. I would teach her lots of stuff, like how to ride a bike."

Caro scans all parts of my face. "Wow, you've thought about this before."

"Yeah. The last year especially."

"Why the last year?"

I shrug. "Maybe because the idea of coming to Australia was starting to take shape. I figure it's something my little sister would've enjoyed."

"The way you talk, it's like you know her. You have a picture of her in your head."

I nod. "You think I'm a drummer short of a marching band now, don't you? You want the cab to pull over so you can get out?"

Caro doesn't reply. She lifts her hand from the seat and places it on top of mine. My heart quakes. My pulse is an avalanche.

She's holding my hand.

She's holding *the* hand.

LET GO!

I jerk out from under the gentle contact and press my arm against my chest. I await the inevitable—shock, anger, cold shoulder. I plow forward.

"Caro, I'm so sorry. I didn't mean to do that. Honestly. It's a reflex thing, nothing at all to do with you. Just a bad…association. I'm so *sorry.*"

Any second now she'll give me the gears.

"I've blown it, haven't I?" I say.

We stop at an intersection. The rain is sheeting down now. A soaked couple in formal dress crosses in front of us, arguing fiercely. Our driver honks the horn, to scold or to egg on—I'm not sure which. I zero in on Caro's face. It's thoughtful, then kind.

"You haven't blown it," she says.

"I'm sorry."

"It's okay, really." She nudges the hair away from my face. "Renee grabbed that hand in the escape room, yeah?"

"Yeah."

She hesitates for a second, then lifts her dress slightly, exposing the outside of her left thigh. Though the light is dim, I can see a nasty scar several inches above the knee.

"A memento from one of my mum's pisshead former boyfriends. One night he tried to glass her. I made sure he didn't." She returns the hem of her dress back to her knees. "I can't hack it when it's touched, even by the doc or the physio. I wear board shorts at the beach. I don't really hate the way it looks; I just hate why it happened." She unclips her seat belt, begins climbing over me.

"What are you doing?"

"Move over. We'll swap sides." After some awkward shuffling—Caro on her feet, me on my backside—we settle into each other's previous spot. She smiles. "This is better, isn't it? We're on our good sides now, as long as you don't have issues with your leftie there."

I shake my head. Our opposite hands now lie flat on the seat, occupying the space between us. The previous gap has been restored.

·········●●·········

Two other things happen on the trip home.

The first—Caro kisses me. On the cheek. Unannounced. Just as the taxi enters the driveway to her house.

Second—she draws a line.

"You've got a bit going on behind those cute blue eyes," she says, exiting the cab to the final spits of the night's downpour. She reaches up to thumb away the lipstick from my face. "A lot, actually."

"That sounds like a *let's just be friends* sort of line," I say glumly.

She leans on the wound-down window. "We are friends. Good friends." She nods toward my hand. "And when you've sorted some stuff out…"

She leaves the sentence unfinished and makes her way to her front door. As she disappears inside, the cab driver asks me where to next.

"Nowhere, I guess."

·········•·········

I press the FaceTime icon. The electronic dolphin noises commence. Vancouver time is just after six in the morning, so maybe it's too early to catch them? No, the *shuck* sound has begun, indicating a pickup. The video feed of my head scuttles up into the corner. My parents' faces appear.

Dad sits to the right of screen, arms loosely folded, face drawn. He's wearing an *E-LIFE* button on the collar of his shirt. Mom looks a bit brighter, but the gloomy, glistening eyes show where she's really at.

"So good to see you, Munro," she says.

"I'm sorry I haven't called before now," I reply. "I'm immersing myself in an *awesome* new culture and having the *rad* adventure I always dreamt about. But that's no excuse."

"It's okay. We've been enjoying the emails."

"Thanks for putting more cash in my account, by the way."

"No problem. You can even keep it if you come home."

I look from Dad to Mom, then back to Dad. Neither is willing to stare down the camera. "Is that the deal? You want me to come home?"

Dad rubs the back of his neck. "We heard from Nina Hyde that there've been a few...challenges at school, so..." He holds both hands up. "Don't get the wrong idea. Whatever you want to do, Munro, we're with you. We want what you want, son."

"Absolutely," adds Mom. "If it's seeing things through, fine. And if it's ending the exchange early, that's okay too. We don't mind."

My parents' faces. Trying not to plead and failing miserably. My mind strays to YVR and the night of my departure. It was like a scene from a Wes Anderson movie—all stilted conversations and uncomfortable silences. Dad kept checking his watch every ten seconds, telling me I shouldn't leave it too late to go through security, there were always delays with security. Mom—she was worse. She drank a doubleshot espresso at Starbucks. She grumbled about the new video for the Foundation's website being too expensive. For the hundredth time that week, she got upset that YOLO had been lax in confirming my pickup details in Brisbane. Neither one said they were second-guessing the decision to let me go. Neither one said they'd be counting the days.

The looks on their faces mirrored the ones I see now.

Go home, Munro. It's what they want. Don't let them down.

Again.

"It's been a bit rocky at school for sure," I say. "But I'm still going, haven't missed a day. I'm in a better headspace now."

I tell them about the volunteering hours, about Fair Go and the Living Partner role. I talk about the Straya Tour and the South Bank trip. I give a brief intro to my team, but I don't mention Blake.

"Sounds like an awesome place," says Mom. "Well suited to your experience." She trails off, then forces a smile. "So how are things with the Hydes? Still going well? They seem to be good people."

"They're great. Not sure they deserve the likes of me, but they're treating me as family."

"That's nice. That's…nice to hear."

Mom begins massaging her forehead. Dad twists the wedding ring on his finger. Outside, I hear the lock open on the front door and footsteps across the floor. Rowan's carefree chatter leaks into my room, followed by Nina's happy cackle.

"It's late over there. We should let you go, I suppose," says Dad. His chin quivers. Mom takes hold of his hand. "We're sorry, Munro. Since Evelyn's passing, we've been too wrapped up in the Foundation, not giving you the things you need here. No wonder you wanted to run away from us."

"Dad, that's not—"

"Let me finish." He nods as if he's been given permission to speak. "We'll make good. We'll be better. That's a promise."

"You don't need to promise anything. You guys aren't the reason I wanted to come here."

"Thank you for saying that."

"It's the truth."

Dad tilts his head. "Be that as it may, we don't want to be the reason you stay." He brings his head back to center and lifts his chin. "Keep at it, son. Keep getting better. And we'll do the same here."

...........●...........

I miss Mom and Dad. And you, of course, Evie.

Can we really be a family? Just the three of us? We have to try. And if it doesn't work? I don't know. I guess we'll always have you.

Why did you have to die, Evie? I think about those kids in the severe-disabilities class. Like Isaac, the boy who had seizures all the time? Or that girl Katie? She couldn't feed herself or go to the bathroom on her own. I mean, I'm not saying you were better than them. It's just...what quality of life do they have? Why are they still alive and you're not?

I'm tired, not thinking straight. Been a long day. A mostly good day. And if my heart doesn't give out, there's another one tomorrow.

Goodnight, Evie.

CHECKESS

Ms. MacGillivray is staring, one eyebrow arched. She has her hands behind her head, pinning her ponytail flat against her skull. The bruise on her right bicep looks like a tiny swirling galaxy. Her teeth are clamped to the butt of a Bic pen.

Mr. Varzani—YOLO program coordinator, student-exchange evaluator, guest of Mother Terrorizer (Ms. Mac has a new derby name)—is also staring, eyes enlarged by thick yellow-tinted lenses surrounded by bold black frames. The Sussex High visitor pass on his shirt pocket is upside down. His pencil hovers over a clipboard.

Both are staring at me, waiting for an answer to their question. I pull a loose thread from the school crest on my shorts.

"I'm enjoying the experience," I say, quoting the YOLO video I watched last night. "I'm trying to make the most of every day, soak it all in. I'm not the same person as when I started, that's for sure."

Mr. Varzani puts his pencil and clipboard down, then applauds. For a split second, I think it will become a standing ovation. "That's brilliant, Munro! That's the sort of spirit we love, right there!"

"Thanks, sir."

"Call me Craig."

"Okay, Craig."

Ms. MacGillivray takes the pen out of her mouth. "How about your midterm marks, Munro—how do you feel about those?"

I tip my hand back and forth. "They're not great, but they're about the same as I had back home. No worse."

"You think it's the best you can do?"

"It is what it is, Miss. I think it's the best I can do in difficult circumstances. The language difference here is a killer."

Craig squints, scratches his ear, then loses it as the joke hits home. His laugh is how I imagine the mating call of a lonely moose. Ms. Mac gives a thin smile. She closes one eye, taking aim again with her guidance gun.

"You in any of the music programs at all, Munro? One of the bands?"

"No."

"Percussion group?"

"No."

"Male choir, perhaps?"

"Only if you want it shut down." I sit up straighter in my seat. "I'm more of a sports guy."

"Well, I see you haven't joined any sports teams either."

"Nothing really stood out."

"Cricket?"

"It's got a million rules, and I know maybe three."

"Rugby?"

"I think I'd rather stay alive."

"What about field hockey?"

"Too difficult in my skates."

Craig moose calls again. I'll cut out the jokes from now on.

"I'm not against joining a sports team, Miss," I add. "It's just that my volunteering is sucking up a lot of time this term."

"You don't have to do all fifty hours before Easter. You've got next term too. Today is March 8, and you've already completed"—Ms. MacGillivray shuffles some papers—"twenty-eight hours. So you're on track to finish by week nine! What's the hurry? What exactly are you doing there, Munro?"

You're still hiding, aren't you. Munro? That's what you're doing. Still thinking you're safe there. But I'm seeking. I'm getting closer. I will find you.

Maybe today?

Seems like the perfect day to bring you out of hiding.

I briefly describe the Living Partner role. I tell them about the Straya Tour (I don't say it's named after me) and our field trips—South Bank, Lone Pine Koala Sanctuary, Bribie Island, the Glass House Mountains. I introduce my team and their latest news: Bernie's still considering names for her clothing line, Iggy has completed a third of his Infecto comic, Flo just taught her first self-defense class, the power couple of Blake and Dale are now calling themselves "Blale," Shah's still sleeping most of the time. Much of the info is over the heads of my audience, but I don't care. Just so long as they get that I prefer volunteering at Fair Go to learning cricket.

"Wow, I remember at the start you didn't want anything to do with the place," says Ms. Mac. "Now you're talking like you're never going to leave."

"Pay's good."

"Funny."

"I'm not gonna lie. I like it there."

She opens her mouth to respond but is blindsided by her YOLO sidekick. For the first time in the meeting, Craig's 'tude is something other than over-the-top cheerleader.

"That's wicked, Munro, but we don't want your volunteer gig being a downer or a bummer for everything else at school," he says, pushing his bumblebee glasses farther up the bridge of his nose. "The sweet zone of a student exchange, as you are aware, is contributing to the host family and school."

"Do you feel Fair Go is being a downer—or perhaps even a bummer—to everything else?" asks Ms. Mac.

I lean forward and point to one of the stats on my midterm report. "What do you see there, Miss?"

"Your attendance? It's perfect."

"That's right. I haven't missed a day yet."

"Just turning up isn't contributing to the school though."

"It's a big improvement from back home. I ditched at DSS. Now I'm a changed man. Do I look like the sort of student who would bail on school? Craig?"

"No student living the true YOLO spirit would dream of such a thing."

"Word. I am nothing if I am not living the true YOLO spirit."

This is all the reassurance Craig Varzani needs. After a glance at his watch, he apologizes, says he must get back to the office. He vows to keep in touch.

"You da man, Munro Maddux," he adds. "I can see great things ahead for you."

Ms. MacGillivray escorts the coordinator to the door. As it closes behind him, she twists her mouth and puts her hands on her hips. Mother Terrorizer might now be in charge.

"Thanks for not telling him about the other stuff, Miss," I say. "The scrums. The freak-outs. Did I miss anything?"

The guidance officer scratches her cheek. "I think you covered it."

"I've kept my nose clean the last two weeks though."

"You have. Indeed, you are...da man, Munro Maddux." She sits down in her chair and grabs a stress ball from her in-tray. She leans back, tossing it from hand to hand. "You're getting better, and Fair Go is playing a big part in that for sure. But you can do more than just volunteering and turning up, mate. Don't be satisfied with better. Go for best."

I wipe my sweaty right palm on my shorts and nod. "Don't you mean *best-er*, Miss?"

....••••••●•••••••....

Caro waits for me at the lockers.

"How was it?" she asks.

"Fine. How are you for time?"

"Still got about twenty minutes left of lunch. What did they say?"

"Nothing much. YOLO guy was a goof. Ms. Mac thinks I should step up." I open my locker, remove the math textbook from my bag, replace it with a single thin folder. "Do the trains west go every half hour or every fifteen minutes?"

"Fifteen minutes."

"Perfect." I close the locker door. "How long's it take to get to the station from here if you run?"

"What's with the questions about the time and the trains, Munro?" Caro's hair-trigger smile, for once, misfires. Her lips stretch. Her face darkens. "You're wagging?"

"Is that the same as ditching? If so, yes, I'm wagging." I hastily add, "But I've got a good reason."

Coward.

I retrieve the folder from my bag, hand it over to Caro. She starts reading the info. "Shah—that's the guy you've been worried about?"

I nod. "We've done, like, four field trips now, and I still haven't been able to get anything out of him. He sleeps when we're on the bus or the train. When we're at the place we're visiting, he wanders around with a scowl on his face, keeping his distance from the group, only speaking when absolutely necessary. The residents are on a rotation for the tour—they decide the places we go. But he won't choose a place."

"So you're going to go see him now?"

"Yeah. He always has Wednesday afternoons off from his work in the residence. I think if I spend some time with him outside of this tour business, that'll give me a better shot at making some progress."

Caro closes the folder and hands it back. She's weighing my rationale, turning it over like an unsolved Rubik's Cube. Caro is serious about school—I learned that about her right away. She's real smart, works hard. She wants marks good enough to go to college and study law. Then she'll practice in human rights or the environment or some other area of standing up to the man—she hasn't quite decided yet. She wants to help the Shahs of the world.

She wants to help herself too. Put the past behind her, including whatever her mom's asshole ex did to scar her leg. We're on the same page, Caro and me. It's just that our books are different: hers is a school text and mine is…I don't know what the hell mine is.

"You know Maeve's auditioning for *The Addams Family* today," she says. "We can still catch it."

"She doesn't care if I'm there or not."

"You could help her care if you showed up. Might help with Digger and Renee too."

I scrunch up my face. "You saying I'm the one who needs to patch things up?"

"Wouldn't hurt."

I check my watch. "Look, I've got better things to do than suck up to those guys. Like practicing chess. That's what Kelvin Yow said I should try with Shah. I'm gonna play some chess with him."

Caro sighs, adjusts her wristbands. "You do remember they take roll in the afternoon, don't you?"

"Yeah."

"So you'll be marked absent."

"Uh-huh."

"And they'll contact Rowan's fam about it."

"Yeah, they send an automated message."

Caro looks down her nose. "It'll take more than your cute accent to talk your way out of that."

"I have a plan."

A group of younger students, probably ninth-graders, swarm the lockers nearby. In voices louder than intended, they're whining about the end of lunch and the start of an English class that isn't "keepin' it real." One boy, a walking goalpost in a droopy uniform and a worn pair of work boots, wonders how reading

Oliver Twist can possibly help him get his "sparky ticket," whatever that is.

"I should go," I say. "Don't suppose you want to come with me?"

Caro scoffs at the unvitation and squeezes my elbow. "You better run if you're going to catch the 12:57."

Caro sees through you.

She's a good person. She knows when people are really doing something to help others and when they're only doing it to help themselves. She knows what you're up to.

You can't hide, Munro.

Not today.

......•••••••••.........

I settle *back into the thin-cushioned seat of the* 12:57 train and put my feet up opposite.

A long line of freight cars fills the window, each one covered in graffiti tags: *NEXST, SNAFU, DOOM, TRAGIC, GEKO!* One detailed work features a hooded figure walking a tightrope. The pole they're carrying for balance has a globe on one end and a miniature of the hooded person on the other. The caption underneath reads *You Decide.*

You haven't answered me for days, Munro. Did Ollie tell you to do that? She's stupid if she did. You can't ignore me. I'm the Coyote.

You can't ignore the people at school either. You think you can run away and no one will find out? They will— of course they will. Then what will you say? Will you tell them why you're running to Fair Go? How you're terrified of the voice in your head? Especially today?

Are you going to tell them?

Answer me, Munro!

ANSWER ME!

..........●..........

It's around 1:50 PM when I ring the bell on the reception desk. Kelvin wanders out from the back room, stapler in hand. We ask the same question of each other in stereo: "What are you doing here?"

Kelvin responds first. "I'm covering the front desk for Laura while she's on lunch. And you? You here for more hours?"

"No." I lower my bag to the scuffed floor, wipe my hands down the front of my Sussex High shirt. "I'm here for school."

"Shouldn't you be *in* school?"

"I am. We have to do a series of interviews with a person of migrant background as part of our diversity project. I thought I would ask you if it's okay to talk to Shah."

Kelvin puts the stapler on the desk, readies a thin stack of paper, smacks the stapler like he's playing whack-a-mole. "Diversity project."

"Yes."

"That would be in…Social Studies?"

"Modern History, actually."

"And you have to interview someone of a different race or ethnicity?"

"Yes."

"Not a gay person? Or an elderly person? Or someone living in poverty?"

"No."

"Not someone with a disability?"

"I guess it's two for one with Shah. But yeah, the question was pretty specific."

Kelvin starts complaining about "hierarchies of difference." I nod at the end of each sentence. This is going well. Kelvin's on a rant that doesn't include the crime of ditching school. I'm glad I didn't go with the extra-hours angle.

"So it's okay if I talk to Shah then?" I ask at the end of the speech, after a suitable respectful pause.

"You should know by now, Munro: it's not my permission you need."

Kelvin picks up the front-desk phone, dials a short number. He waits and waits. And waits. He starts singing the theme song to *The Big Bang Theory*. After at least a full minute, he says, "Hi, Shah, sorry to wake you… You have a visitor…Munro Maddux…Munro, your Living Partner…Well, he's sixteen—I wouldn't call him a 'boy'…Yes, he's here…Yes, it's Wednesday…Yes, it's not the usual time…He wants to do an interview with you… An interview…For school…" Kelvin holds his hand over the phone. "He's thinking about it."

I bend forward, rest my elbows on the counter. Not going quite as well now. The idea that Shah might not want to play ball—I didn't really factor that in. How could he turn this down? Just the two of us, hanging out at home, no tourism in the way?

"Tell him we could play chess too," I say. "If he wants."

"Munro says you and him could play chess…You don't want to play chess?…You *hate* chess?…You want to play checkers instead."

"We can do that."

Kelvin says "uh-huh" four times in quick succession, then hangs up the phone. "He says you can visit provided you don't try and pretend you know anything about football."

"I think I can manage that."

We exit reception and follow the winding walkway that is Fair Go's main artery. Flowers of many colors line the path. One looks like a red hairbrush and is attractive to the local bees. The path cuts through what Kelvin calls the business district: the Creative Arts Precinct, the Recycling Depot, the Digital Media Center. Looking in the windows of the buildings, I hope to see glimpses of my team in action. I'm disappointed. The beating heart of Fair Go is still a mystery to me. I got a sense of it at my interview and on my orientation, but it's been all bus rides and Brisbane sights since then. Ironic, I think. I'm touring the city and beyond, but the place I'd really like to see remains under wraps.

"So you're missing a class to be here, correct?" asks Kelvin as we approach the boxy, red-brick townhouses.

"Yeah."

"Generous of Sussex to allow you to do that. Are there other students getting this deal too?"

"I don't know."

He checks his watch. "Is there a form I need to sign? Or someone I need to call? You know, to confirm that you turned up and weren't wagging?"

"There's no form."

We enter the Living Precinct and walk along the pavers-on-gravel path to the front door of House 4. Kelvin knocks, then cups his ear against the door. The welcome mat at our feet is turned over. We wait for ages, then finally hear footsteps. Locks are released.

The door opens slowly, revealing Shah's retreating figure. Before he disappears, I get a look at the back of his head. He's had a haircut—a hair chop, in fact. The close shave highlights the dent in the lower part of his skull. It's pink and stark and impossible to ignore. It's like an unblinking eye.

Kelvin extends an open hand toward the inside of House 4.

"Best of luck with the interview, Munro."

........●..........

Shah and I sit on either side of a small table, chessboard set up for play.

"You don't want to play checkers after all, Shah, eh?"

"Yes. I do."

"Oh. Do you have the right pieces?"

"These here, they are good."

"You want to play checkers with chess pieces?"

"Yes. You have problem with that?"

"No, no…not at all. Do you want to get started?"

"I am not ready."

"Okay, cool. No probs."

I look around the living space. It's quite the pad, everything a young resident could want: TV, sound system, couch and chairs. There's even a foldaway treadmill in one corner. The contrast between here and what I've seen in the worker areas is glaring. The staff residences are pretty basic. The fridge in the break room has a loose handle. The furniture in Kelvin's office— I'd bet on most of it being secondhand. The phone in reception is one of those bricks they were making before I was born.

"Sweet setup you have here, Shah. You must like having all this good stuff."

"These things…they are not mine."

"Well, okay, you didn't buy them. But you live here. This is your home."

"This is not my home."

I look around again, this time recognizing what's not here. The meaningful, nonmaterial things. Photos, artwork, maybe a small flag or some cultural knick-knacks. There is a colourful mat—I'm guessing for prayer—spread out beside the armchair.

"Do you always feel that way?" I ask.

"Is this the interview for your school now?"

"Um, sort of. More just a chat at this point."

"You want to know why I like to sleep very much?"

"Sorry?"

"For interview. You want to know why I like to sleep very much?"

I shrug. "If you want to tell me, sure."

Shah takes the white queen in a pincer grip and begins twisting the piece this way and that. His Adam's apple shifts in his throat.

"When I am awake, I think about my family. Are they hopeful? Are they sad? Are they even still alive? Were they killed because they help me to escape civil war and the camp? I think about them when I am awake in the back of truck that take me out of city and across Pakistan border. On the boat crossing ocean from Indonesia. In detention on Nauru. In Australia after I finally processed as proper refugee after ten months. And I think about them today, when I am here at Fair Go."

He releases the white queen, aims and flicks the piece with his middle finger. It skitters across the board, falls over and rolls through a couple of black pawns. It comes to a stop beside one of the black bishops.

"When I sleep," he continues, "I don't think about my family—I am *with* my family. We are together. I talk to them. They talk to me. And everything is good, everything is correct...until I am awake again."

I let Shah's words take as much air as they need. For a while after Evie died, it was the opposite for me. I didn't want to sleep. I would replay the whole scene in my dreams—the collapse, the panic, the compressions, the numb nausea as the paramedics took her away. There was always something different in the replay, some awful alteration of the facts. It might be her eyes being open or her lips being yellow or her chest disintegrating under the weight of my hands. One time, we exchanged places. It was the only dream where I woke up sweating instead of the usual shivering.

Sleep got a bit better when the decision was made to come to Australia. Waking hours? They're still hard, but the Fair Go effect is spreading. To twist Shah's words, more and more I am without the Coyote. We aren't together. I don't talk to it. It doesn't talk to me. And everything is good, everything is correct.

Never thought I'd feel that way, today of all days. March 8.

I place the white queen in the palm of my hand and offer it to Shah. "I don't want to stay too long. I want to let you get back to sleep. But before I go, let's play some checkers, eh?"

Our eyes lock—for how long, I'm not sure. Then he reaches out, grasps the queen, returns it to its proper place on the board.

"I knew how to play chess before I am in detention center," he says. "I cannot remember anything about game now. It is too hard."

We begin playing checkers. Diagonal shifts, one space at a time, an occasional jump, staying true to our team squares. We're about a dozen moves in when I flip the script and use one of my knights to capture a white pawn two spaces across and one down. Shah gives a short, sharp shake of the head, like he just chugged some foul medicine.

"What are you doing? You can't do that."

I facepalm, move the knight back. "Ah, sorry. Forgot what we were playing there for a second. Been spending a ton of time lately practicing chess. Knights can move in an L shape."

We continue. Take a piece here, give a piece there. Shah rides a bishop all the way to the end zone and crowns it with a bottle cap. A cheer from somewhere near the Rec Refuge comes through the window. Maybe our matchup is being broadcast to the rest of the village. I move a rook four spaces across and kick Shah's other bishop to the curb.

"What is this?"

"I can do that, can't I?"

"No! You cannot!"

"Sorry, dude. Totally thought that was allowed in chess *and* checkers. My bad."

Shah glares at me. For a second I'm worried he's going to quit the game. Get up, storm off, tell me to leave and never come back. If he's thinking all of it—any of it— the thoughts are short-lived. He kings a pawn with a small rusty nut.

"I have excuse for dumb play," he says, a hint of friendly teasing in his tone. "What is yours?"

"Hockey hits," I reply.

The contest marches to the finish line. Twenty minutes after we started, Shah has four pieces left, two kinged; I have three and two. It's my turn. One decisive move will tip the balance in this checkers game, and I have one ready, but it's not meant to claim victory. I grab the black king and send it in all directions, sweeping the board, leaving a single white pawn as the lone survivor. Shah bursts out laughing.

"You had *many* hockey hits, yes?" he asks.

"Whassup?"

"The king, he cannot move like that. Only the queen."

"Say that again?"

"The king cannot move everywhere. The queen, yes; the king, no."

I stare at Shah as I return his pieces to their previous positions. His laugh has faded into a smile and more of his first language. I wait for the puck to drop. It doesn't. He has no clue what he just said, doesn't get that he remembered. Should I tell him? As much as I want to, I can't be sure he'd be cool about it. And I don't want to jeopardize this afternoon's progress. For now, maybe it's best to let it slide. The fact that the memories are still there—that's good enough.

An image jumps to mind: the back of Shah's head, whole, complete, no chunk missing.

We play the game out. I stick to checkers the rest of the way. Shah wins (fair and square—I didn't tank) and, after a rejected high five and a reset of the board, I tell him I should bounce so he can go back to sleep.

"Same time next week, if it's okay with you?"

"For more interview or more checkers?"

"Whatever you want."

"For hockey hits," he says. "And talking to you is good. It makes me want more sleep."

I grin and head for the door. On the way out, I sneak one last peek at my stated reason for ditching school. Shah is sitting back in his chair, arms folded, surveying the chessboard like it's something he built with his own hands.

...........●...........

When I get home, Hyde husband and wife are sitting on the front deck.

"Hey, Munro," says Nina. "How was school?"

"Good."

"You came home late today, yeah?"

"I wanted to get some homework out of the way."

"Nice!"

"Come inside, mate," says Geordie. "We'd like to have a quick word, if that's okay."

"Um, sure."

We get comfortable in the living room. I glance at the phone, then zero back in on the Hydes. There's no suggestion they're aware of my bailout. No vibe of anger or disappointment. Just sympathy and concern.

"We won't beat around the bush," says Geordie. "We wanted to talk to you about this Fair Go place."

"Okay."

"About the work you're doing there."

They exchange a solemn look, then Geordie leans forward, elbows on his knees, hands interlocked.

"You've been talking a lot about one of the residents in particular. Zahd? Zar?"

"Shah."

"That's him. Shah. Can you tell us a bit more about him?"

I study Geordie's craggy face. Still no alarm bells. "He's from Afghanistan. He's had a lot of problems since he had to leave his country, one of which is a head trauma that might have happened along the way. I can't say for sure. Anyway, it's the reason he's at Fair Go. He's sad and angry, and he wants to sleep all the time so he can dream about being back with his family. And he can't remember things the way he used to, like chess, for example. That's where I'm trying to assist him, helping him remember how to play chess."

Geordie gets up, begins pacing the rug. He tucks his hands into the pockets of his khakis. A vein has appeared on his forehead. "Sounds like you're on a bit of a mission with him."

"I guess you could say that."

"One that you might want to continue after your fifty hours' volunteering is up?"

"I haven't really thought about it. I guess I could."

Geordie stops, gives a look to his wife that says *your turn* and sits on the coffee table.

"Munro, it's wonderful what you're doing out there," says Nina. "This Shah fellow is lucky to have you taking an interest in him. But we're both a bit worried that… well, that you're getting in a bit deep. We want you to go to Sussex State High, work hard, have fun and take home the best experience possible. We don't want you to go home disappointed that…that Shah didn't remember how to play chess."

"I won't go home disappointed," I reply. "I'm going to a good school. I've made new friends. I've got a great family taking care of me. Fair Go is a bonus. It's gravy. Yes, I like helping Shah and the other residents. But I'm not expecting miracles. I've got everything in perspective."

Liar.

Geordie pats the coffee table, and I sit beside him. He studies my face top to bottom, as if it's a map of a place he's never seen. I wonder if he's imagining me behind a car window, panic-stricken, water rising all around.

"Helping a young man like Shah—that's a good thing, Munro. A very good thing. No two ways about it." His voice is barely above a whisper. "But here's the rub: you can only do so much to make things right."

He lays a hand on my shoulder. It's heavy and stiff.

"After that, you need to help yourself."

Ah, but it's March 8.

You helped yourself just fine today, didn't you?

··········●●●··········

Louis talks through a FaceTime delay and a mouthful of breakfast poutine. "Sounds *too* easy, bro. What's the catch?"

"No catch."

"Nothing?"

"Nope."

"The Hydes will find out you're cutting classes eventually, man. Then they'll tell your mom and dad."

"First off, it's only Wednesday afternoons. Second, it's not really cutting. Third, Mom and Dad said they'd support me whatever I wanted to do."

Lou points a soggy fry down the line. "Dude, sounds like you're trying to convince yourself rather than me."

"It's the truth."

"Truth, eh? That's all I want—gimme some. Just like Eddie Vedder says." He pushes his half-empty bowl aside, wipes his hands down the front of his shirt. His face goes all sucked lemon. "So gimme the truth about today, bro."

"What about it?"

"March 8? One-year anniversary of Evie's death? Is that the real reason for all this cutting business?"

I shrug. "Just another day, man. Just another number on the calendar."

Louis's reply is disrupted by a knock on the bedroom door. Rowan pokes his head in.

"Sorry, Lou. I gotta go."

My best friend since elementary school gives me a minor hairy eyeball and wags a finger. "To be continued, Mr. Maddux."

"Or not, Mr. Teen Helpline."

My tablet screen blanks out. I wave for Rowan to come in.

"Sorry, Mun. Didn't mean to interrupt."

"This is your house—you don't have to be sorry."

"Yeah, well, I might get kicked out with the sneaky shit you've got me doing." He laughs at my instant horror.

"I'm kidding, brother!" He thumbs through one of the old surf mags on the TV stand. "So you probably worked it out from your chat with the oldies—I wiped the phone message the school sent. They don't have a clue."

"Thanks, man."

"And I can keep wiping them, if you want."

"I don't want to get you in trouble."

"Meh. As far as my criminal record goes, this is littering." Rowan sits in the office chair at the desk and spins slowly. "A message will probably get through to the 'keeper at some point though. You know that, hey?"

"Yeah."

"You be able to handle the fallout?"

"I guess we'll find out when it happens." I shift up to the head of my bed and slip a pillow behind my back. "Can I ask you something?"

"Go for it."

"Why are you good with this? Okay, I get that to you it's littering, but why are you helping me?"

Rowan stops spinning. He rubs his buzz-cut head.

"Do you know exactly what went down with Dad's rescue?"

"No."

"You didn't look it up out of curiosity?"

"No."

"Didn't search any of the million articles out there?"

I fold my arms. "Evie's death was a story too, so I know what it's like to have your misery out there. And there is misery in Geordie's rescue, isn't there?"

Rowan blows a big puff of breath and begins talking to the ceiling.

"January 11, 2011, at the height of the flood, Dad tied a rope around his waist and swam out to a blue Ford Fiesta caught in the Logan River. He pulled the driver out—a man named Patrick Cloutier—and managed to drag him back to the bank. Then he swam out again to get Patrick's brother, Sean. He was in the passenger seat. Dad was about halfway out when the car got swept away. Sean's body was found the next day near the Carbrook golf course."

Rowan covers his mouth and coughs. In the corner, something is loose inside the guts of the pedestal fan, sticking with each rotation.

"A lot of stuff happened in the three years after that, up until Dad left work on medical. Not much of it was good. Not even the medals. The thing I remember most about those three years is the look Dad had most of the time. Sort of uptight, distracted. It was like he was still in the water, still with the rope tied around him. Waiting. Waiting for that blue Fiesta to come back so he could finish the job. Waiting for a chance to make things right."

He brings his gaze down and flips it my way.

"I've seen that look on you, brother. First day you were here, quite a few days since. In the scraps. At Liber8. When you got caught in the train door at Wattle Ridge. Even around here. It's not fun seeing that look. And sure as shit, I know it's not fun living with it. So I'm trying to help you get rid of it."

···········•●•···········

Mom and Dad:

My March 8 has just ended and yours is just starting. Hard to believe it's been one year. I considered FaceTiming, but I bailed. Thought it might make things harder rather than easier.

I was okay today. Better than okay, actually. In my interview with the YOLO *coordinator, he said he can see great things ahead for me(!) And do you remember me telling you about my team at Fair Go? You remember Shah? I made a pretty big breakthrough with him. I played "checkess" with him—a combo of chess and checkers. It helped bring back some memories he'd lost. School was fine too, btw. The afternoon class was particularly good. I haven't had any major "challenges" the last couple of weeks.*

March 8 will always be hard. What I did today— it didn't make things easier, but it made things better. And if things keep getting better, they'll eventually be the best they can be. That's what I'm aiming to do. Not just March 8. Every day.

When you visit Evie's grave today, tell her I love her and I miss her.

M

FAIR GO

The three weeks before Easter break were the best three weeks I'd had since Evie's death. The Straya Tour went to Mount Glorious, the State Library and Suncorp Stadium for a football match. With each trip, the Living Partner role felt more and more like a second skin. I began to get hugs goodbye, saved seats on the bus, rabbit ears in photos. It was all unicorns and double rainbows. Mostly anyway. Florence started calling me "Mr. Wrong" due to my ongoing avoidance of a right-handed thumb-wrestling bout. Iggy kept insisting the license plate on the bus be changed so it was more difficult to track. Shah was still largely a nonfactor. The Afghani refugee was awake much of the time though. I'd like to think our

Wednesday afternoons playing checkess had something to do with it.

Caro and I spent a lot of time together. We were still in the friend zone, but that didn't stop Rowan's labeling us "Thunder and Lightning." Back home, the Foundation had its best month to date, in large part because the new video got some run on CTV *Morning Live* and *Breakfast Television*.

Last but definitely not least, the Fair Go effect reached Sussex State High.

A lock-down drill came and went without my needing a paper bag to breathe into. A couple of meathead rugby players who suggested I should *go back to America* got a reply of *With yo mama?* instead of a physical confrontation. I still got the odd token twinges in my chest and my right hand, but there were no full-on freezes, no vivid flashbacks.

No Coyote.

Well, almost. I hardly heard a peep out of him, a comment here, a question there, mostly mailed in. It was more a whisper than a voice. It was the clearest evidence yet of improvement. It was nailing the first four letters in the word *goodbye*.

Of course, because the life of Munro Maddux could never be completely stress free, there was still the odd fire to put out.

The first was sparked by **YOLO**. After a routine check-in with my parents, they beefed up the backgrounder in my Sussex student-exchange profile. The add? Mom's "pity poor Munro" email sent along with my original application.

"I promise it totally stays on the down low," Craig Varzani assured me, and a cringe crawled across my face.

On March 16, Ms. Mac interrupted Geography to summon me to a one-on-one meeting. As we strode in silence toward her office, I wondered what she was thinking. Was she upset that I'd deceived her? Mad? Would she bodycheck me, send me flying? Slameron Diaz certainly had the chops to do it. I risked a look in her direction as we passed the 2011 tribute mural. No bruises or scratches. I didn't know if it was an omen.

We entered her office. There was a new poster on the wall: *Don't ask me nothing and I won't tell you no lies. —Anonymous.* Seemed appropriate. I took a seat. Across from me, Ms. Mac pondered, elbows on the desk, hands joined, tips of her fingers tapping out Morse code.

"You've been through a lot, Munro," she began.

"It's in the past, Miss," I replied.

"Is it?"

"Yeah, it is. Evie died over a year ago. I'm here in Australia. I'm enjoying the student exchange. I'm trying to go for best and not be satisfied with better."

"You sure about that?"

"Absolutely."

Ms. Mac mulled things over. The clock on the wall checkmarked my performance so far: *tick...tick...tick... tick...*

"I do have to talk to your teachers about this."

"*Talk*...what does that mean?"

"It means they need to be informed."

"How informed?"

"What info do you reckon they should have?"

"None."

"Because it's in the past?"

"I want it to stay that way."

Ms. MacGillivray nodded once, in slow motion. She suggested telling the teachers that I'd "experienced family difficulties" and "may require some special consideration." Could I handle that? I said I could.

"There's one more thing," she added. "I think you should seriously think about getting some help, Munro."

"Sorry?"

"If 'best' is truly your goal, someone should be giving you a helping hand while you're here." Ms. Mac rose, rounded the desk, dropped down to her haunches beside my chair. "There's a couple of really good people I could recommend, folks who work with young people doing it tough. I could give you their numbers, email addresses."

"I'm already in contact with a teen helpline on a regular basis," I said. "And just so's you know, I'm able-bodied. Regular brain. No third copy of chromosome 21. No hole in the heart." I nodded. "I am *the helping hand*."

The second fire was no inferno, but still needed to be put out. Caro and Rowan must've been on the gang about their bad case of Munro-itis, because they all came after me. In class, at lunch, after school, individually and together. Even Renee got in on the act. No longer could I practice chess or research popular T-shirt designs or read comics with obscure superheroes or check out stories of special-needs marriages or watch videos of made-up martial-arts moves. They would find me and befriend me, regardless of how I felt about it.

There was plenty of news to update. Maeve's high-light of the school fete was Rowan's cooking—specifi-cally, a batch of "to-die-for honey-and-fig bikkies" he made for the bake sale. Renee passed around her list of heckles for the opening night of *The Addams Family* (Maeve would be spared any burns). Digger revealed that the pursuit of Jessica Mauboy as his semiformal date was going to plan. He'd favorited two hundred of her tweets since January. The magic number was three hundred, and then he would pop the question via DM.

I knew they weren't really reaching out to me—they were just doing it to make Caro and Rowan happy. But I played along. That made Caro and Rowan happy too.

The third fire to be extinguished was lit by my parents.

We'll be visiting with you soon!

That was the opening line in the email that arrived March 21. The lines that came after it were just as WTF.

Nina and Geordie invited us to come over and visit. They felt you were a bit homesick and thought you could do with a familiar face (or two!). We were delighted to accept the invitation, and I'm looking at flights as I write this!

I won't lie—a big part of me wanted them to come. A bigger part, though, was fearful about what might happen if they did. I was progressing, I had momentum. Would it come to a screeching halt with my parents around? Would the Coyote find new life with Mom and Dad on the scene? I didn't want to find out.

I FaceTimed them on March 22. Dad sensed what was coming and the sort of message I was bringing. His first comment came down the line before the video feed had even kicked in.

"You don't want us there, do you, Munro?"

His face appeared. He'd grown a beard since the last call, a patchy, scraggly excuse for a goatee. The bags under his eyes could've carried groceries.

"I do, but I…don't. I'm sorry, Dad."

He sniffed and looked off to the side. "What did I tell you, Belinda? You owe me twenty bucks."

Mom entered the fray. She was wearing pajamas and carrying a hot drink, probably one of her Zen teas.

"Quit it, Malcolm! We did not bet!" She turned to me. "There was no bet, Munro."

"I know it's a joke, Mom."

"Honey, we'd love to see you."

"You're seeing me now."

"We'd love to see you *in person*. I think a short visit would be great for all of us. We could meet the Hyde family and see some sights and…you know, just spend some time together, without the pressure of the past or the future. Just enjoy a few moments in the present. Munro?"

Tears pooled in Mom's lower lids. Her twenty-four-hour delight over the Hydes' invite had been crushed underfoot. Was I being cruel? Was I blowing the idea out of the water before at least giving it a chance to float? Ollie might have applied one of her labels to me: joy bomber.

People who've been through serious shit, she'd said, *can really struggle to accept nice things happening to them or around them. Instead of appreciation, they nuke it with anger or cynicism or disdain or just something negative. They joy-bomb it.*

I wasn't joy-bombing my parents. Joy-slapping, yes; joy-punching, maybe. Definitely not joy-bombing. I leaned in closer to the propped iPad, but looked toward my suitcase, standing in the corner of the bedroom like a bodyguard.

"Coming over," said Dad. "We just thought it would help dispel some of our fears."

"How many do you have?"

"A ton. Losing you. The future. Whether we're doing the right thing. Whether the exchange will help you heal. Just to name a few. All of them are real to us." Dad tapped his forehead several times, perhaps trying to loosen up his memory. "The night you left, son, after you went through security, your mom and I wanted to sit down, so we went to a bar near the check-in area. It was about nine thirty; the place closed at ten, so there was time for a drink or two. But we didn't want to drink. We didn't want to watch the game on the TVs. Didn't even want to talk. We just sat there, gawking at the procession of late-night travelers, looking like we'd lost a fortune on a coin flip. Eventually, a waiter had to ask us to leave because they were closing up. I was reluctant to go. Mom had to take my elbow and lead me out. I think there was something about the act of leaving, the actual passing through the doors of the terminal, that felt wrong to me, like an ending I couldn't understand.

"On the drive home, Mom asked me, *Are you regretting the decision to let Munro go away?* I pulled the car over to the shoulder and searched for an answer. It took a while. *Munro went away the day his sister died*, I said. *I don't know how to bring him back*."

Mom closed her eyes, let her head fall to the side.

"We still don't know how to bring you back, son," added Dad. "I guess we're still trying. That's why we jumped at the chance to come over and visit. But, just as it is with Evie, we have to understand we *can't* bring you back. I can't, Mom can't, your sister can't, God up in Heaven can't. Only *you* can bring Munro Maddux back. We need to get that. But it seems we're not there yet."

The following day, Nina showed me an email Mom had sent:

Hi, Nina:

Thank you so much for your very kind invitation—unfortunately, we will now have to pass. There are some things with our work at the Foundation that we have been unable to shift.

Thank you again for all you are doing to take care of our Munro.

Sincerely,
Belinda Maddux

Three fires doused amid three weeks of awesome. And now I've arrived at the first morning after the Easter long weekend, the first proper opportunity to tour the only place in Brisbane I really want to see. The failing grip of the Coyote is set to give out altogether.

I turn away from the Fair Go Welcome sign and motion for Caro to join me. "You ready to Living Partner like a boss?"

She smiles and adjusts her black wristbands. "Lead the way."

·········●●··········

"Caro, this is Kelvin Yow. He's the residential manager."

"Thank you for having me here."

"No worries. The residents who work with Munro are the ones you should thank. Normally, they would have a face-to-face before letting you loose, but they made an exception in your case. A thumbs-up from Mr. Maddux here is good enough for them."

"I tried to warn them," I add. "I said you were a horrible person, really mean, not too bright, bad hygiene."

Caro shrugs. "All true."

"They said they didn't mind—working with me, they were used to it."

"Well, I'm not," says Kelvin. "So how about we get you two awful teenagers out and about."

On the walk to the Creative Arts Precinct, Caro notices everything: the ramp accesses, the park benches, the hand-carved *Wally Yow Way* street sign. She also has a hundred questions for Kelvin: How long has Fair Go been around? How many residents? How many staff? What sort of activities do you do? What sort of support do you provide? In many cases, she already knows the answers, either from talking to me or from her own research. By the time we reach the studio door (painted with the image of a mermaid on a swing), Kelvin has a solid opinion of Caro, one I've heard before. He shares it with me quietly, behind a cupped hand. "She's a keeper, Munro."

Before leaving, he makes sure we're set for the day: basic map, schedules, mobile-phone numbers. He looks at our shoes.

"Ah, good, you've got your runners on. The residents have planned a little something for you this afternoon."

"It's not another field trip, is it?" I ask. "I mean, the touring is great, but that's all we've been doing. I really want to stick around home here."

"You're staying here, mate, but it is touring...for the residents. They're looking to get a little taste of your homeland." Kelvin smiles and brings an index finger to his lips. "I'll say no more. Enjoy yourselves today, and I'll catch you this arvo at the Shed."

After Kelvin departs, Caro bumps me with a little hip check.

"What was that for?" I ask.

"You called this place *home*—that's really sweet."

........●..........

Seven weeks. Seven stops. Barbecues and beaches, theme parks and theaters, rugby games and rainforests. I've listened, played, occasionally guided. I've done it all without the Coyote in my ear. The Straya Tour has been great, but I've also felt shielded, kept inside a nice busy bubble, away from the real action. It's left me wanting more. It's left me wanting the true Fair Go. That's what I expect to find today.

In the Creative Arts Precinct, those expectations take flight. Every part of the scene stokes the smile on my face: the colors, the materials, the humming machines, the buzzing voices. The people. Smiling, laughing. Working together. Singing along to the tune tumbling out of the Bose speakers—"Dangerous Woman" by Ariana Grande. A girl sits in a wheelchair made to look like an ice-cream truck. A young guy wearing an eye patch darts about taking photos of finished pieces on display. "Etsy will love this!" he announces after each snap, as if Etsy is a favorite aunt. A girl seated in a La-Z-Boy off to the side looks like she's opting out of the action. A closer look shows she's putting together a bracelet that has *LUKE* spelled out in beads. The place is a beauty. A sign on one of the walls has a message in an ornate font: *Art is education, art is vocation, art is therapy...art is LIFE!*

"How great is this?" says Caro, examining the school of glass tropical fish hanging from the ceiling.

"It's something else," I reply.

Bernie appears from a small nook near the screen-printing area and scurries over. She's blinking at regular speed, but the rest of her is pumped. Hands flicking, mouth twitching. Her cheeks are redder than cherry Kool-Aid.

"Munro, I'm so glad you're here!"

"Bernie, I'd like to introduce you to someone."

"I've figured it out!"

"This is Caro."

"The word for my clothing line!"

"She's my friend."

"After all this time, I've finally got it!"

Caro holds out her hand, but it's left hanging. I click my fingers. "Caro's saying hi." For a few seconds Bernie is thrown. She tucks her elbows into her hips and hunches forward, trying to gather my words to her chest. Then she turns and stares at the hand suspended in midair.

"Lovely to meet you, Bernie. Munro has told me heaps about you."

Bernie makes a fist and pushes it into her chin. "I'm very sorry," she says, staring at Caro's sneakers. "I was a bit excited and forgot my social skills. Munro and I have been working on this for a while."

"It's been all you, Bern." I lean to the side. "In your back pocket—is that one of your new shirts?"

Bernie snaps her head up and stands tall. The hunch in her back (I've learned that it's called a kyphosis) shrinks and flattens. She plucks the T-shirt from her pocket and lays it across her extended forearms.

"*Freetard*? That's the word you came up with?"

She nods enthusiastically. "It's someone who doesn't use the R-word. And Freetard changes the bad word to something good. I've done shirts in my three favorite fonts: Forte, Impact and Helvetica. This is the Forte one."

"It's eye-catching," I say. "Do you think it could be taken the wrong way though?"

"How?"

"Well, people might see Freetard as a different sort of insult."

Bernie gives a big belly laugh. "No way, Jose! It changes the bad word to something good. Duh!"

"I think it's great," says Caro. "Where can I buy one?"

"You can have this one. I'll give you a cap too, when we start making them." Bernie looks me up and down. "I think you should have an Impact shirt, Munro."

"Okay, sure." I hitch a thumb over my shoulder toward the bustling studio. "How can we help out this inefficient, poorly run hater operation?"

Bernie balks, then pulls a face. "Joking, ha!" She plunges her hands in her pockets and looks around. "Hmm. Everyone understands the equipment and the rules and what to do. The Fair Go Working Partners have more responsibility for things backstage, as they say, like buying materials and getting donations. If we get something new in the studio—like our new kiln over there—they teach us how to use it. I s'pose you could come over and help me with screen printing?"

Under the careful watch of Bernadette Polk, Caro and I spend the rest of our scheduled hour making Freetard shirts. Like everyone else in the studio, we laugh and sing and display our work for the Etsy photographer. When the time comes to end our "shift," it hurts a little to leave.

Good thing First Aid is next.

..........●●..........

We arrive to find Iggy looking at letters he's scribbled on his hand.

"*D-R-A-B-C*," he says. "You know what that means."

I nod. "*Danger, response, airway, breathing, circulation.*"

"You and I both hope you'll never need CPR, Munro. But if you do, and I'm here, I'll do it, and I'll do it well. You're in good hands. I'll even shake on it."

"You stealing my speeches now, Ig?" I say, laughing and accepting his offered elbow.

At the front of the class, the instructor is talking quietly to himself, prepping the session. I recognize him from the day of my interview.

"The guy up front running the show…is his name Percy?"

Iggy shakes his head. "Perry. Perry Richter. He's good. Very smart."

"He's not a resident, is he?"

"No. He just comes here to teach."

"First aid. And car washing, yeah?"

"And nuclear physics."

"Did you just make a joke?"

"Yes."

"Not bad."

Iggy smiles and resumes the study of his palm. This is the best I've seen him. No coughs or throat clears, no cool washcloths or warm blankets, no sickly voice. No darting looks for suspicious strangers. There's a bit of sunburn on his nose. I'm not surprised. First thing he said to me today was, "My comic! I'm three quarters done!" The way he's going, he'll be doing cartwheels and one-arm push-ups at the finish.

"So does Perry teach the group on his own?" I ask.

"Yes."

"No Working Partner?"

Iggy points out a bald, bearded guy with a tattoo sleeve, counting bandages off to the side of the room. "Baz is always here. He helps with putting stuff out and cleaning up. And he's a really good victim for practicing. But he doesn't teach."

"Perry's got a certificate or something?"

"Yeah, he shows it to us at the beginning of each class."

"He sounds perfect for the job," says Caro.

Iggy nods. "He has real-life experience too. He saved his sister by giving her cardiopulmonary resuscitation. It must be true, 'cause he kept saying, *No lie!* all the time."

Iggy tells the story. Earthquakes, car stunts, a mad dash to the hospital…it sounds more like a movie than something that actually happened. I don't feel great as I listen in—my heart's jumped up a level and my stomach is a bit watery—but I don't feel ambushed. I know where I am. I know *who* I am.

Caro tugs my shirt sleeve. "You with us, Munro? You okay?"

I scan the room. Residents take up their positions, and Perry Richter calls for attention. "Hello, everyone. As my father used to say, what do we want? No more delays! When do we want it? As soon as possible! That's a good joke."

"I'm fine," I say, patting Caro's hand. "Let's get hurt."

Arms are broken. Legs are stabbed. Systems go into shock. People turn into mummies, bandaged in head dressings and figure-eight wraps and collar-and-cuff slings. Perry is as good as advertised, clear in his steps and in his demos on Baz the victim. He sees everything that's happening in the room, even when he's looking to the side or at his fingernails. He talks about Jackie Chan, injuries he suffered, films on which they occurred. At the end of the session, he approaches us, holding a batch of *DRABC* pocket cards and a small green dome.

"Hello, my name is Perry Richter," he says, fanning the cards so we can each grab one. "Thank you for coming today, and you too, Iggy, even though you are here all the time."

"I'm Caro. It was an awesome class, Perry. Everyone was totally into it."

"Thank you, Caro."

"Yeah, you rocked it," I say. "By the way, I'm—"

"Munro Maddux, the young person from the excellent city of Vancouver, home of the Qube building and Stanley Park and the PNE." Perry dips his head to one side and flutters his half-closed eyes. "You are here on a student exchange."

"That's right. How did you know?"

"Kelvin Yow told me about you and said you would be here today." He flicks his fingers. "I would like to talk to you alone, please."

"Alone?"

He turns to Caro and fixes his gaze on the Rip Curl badge on her cap. "I'm sorry, Caro, it is not great manners to take Munro away to talk."

"Go for it."

"Thank you."

Perry moves toward the front of the room, where a CPR mannequin is laid out on a table, awaiting pickup from Baz. I shrug and make my way over. We end up on either side of the mannequin, which is named Annie, according to the nearby storage bag.

"Were you comfortable in my class today, Munro?" asks Perry.

I glance at Caro and Iggy. They're watching something on Caro's phone and laughing. "I felt very comfortable, Perry."

"No lie?"

"Um, no. No lie. It was great to be a part of this session."

Perry squints. "Excellent! Kelvin told me that you might not be comfortable in the class this morning. He did not say why." He puts the small green dome down on the table, beside Annie, and gives it a pat. "I didn't feel anything in my seismometer here, in the lead-up or during the class."

"That's...good." I stare at Annie's lifeless face. "Iggy told me about your sister. It's awesome that you saved her life."

Perry makes a *pop* sound with his mouth. "It is. I couldn't save my parents though. My father died from pancreatic cancer two weeks before my twin sister and I turned eighteen. My mother died of lung cancer last spring. Now it's just me and Justine and her husband, Marc, and their baby, Daniel Leon Richter. He's my nephew. No lie, it would be very good if my parents were still alive, but they're not, so I try to make things very good without them."

"I imagine that's hard to do."

"It is hard to do, but that is today, that is the future." He scrunches his eyes and sucks in a big breath. He lays a hand on the seismothingy. "You are positive you felt comfortable in my class this morning?"

"One hundred and ten percent."

Perry scoffs. "That's not possible!"

He says goodbye, waves to Caro and Iggy, then exits. I wander back to the pair.

"Good chat?" asks Caro.

I nod. "It was. No lie."

...............●..............

After a quick lunch in the cafeteria, Caro and I crash the personal-safety talk at the Rec Refuge. A Working Partner named Darrell is in charge. His subject for today is online dangers—specifically, ransomware. As he outlines the best course of action—"Whatever you do, do *not* pay anything to these people!"—Caro notices a second instructor readying for her bit.

"Is that Florence?"

"Yep."

"There's not much to her."

I nod. "She's real strong though."

Caro rubs her hands together like an evil mastermind. "I've been looking forward to this. What's that move you said she was showing the others at Bribie?"

"The Blue-Ringed Octopus Bite. I think Iggy's still recovering."

Darrell passes on his final bit of ransomware advice: "Whatever you do, do *not* pay anything to these people!", then motions for Florence to join him at the front. "Okay, to finish up, folks, as per usual we have our resident ninja goddess, Florence, here to teach you her self-defense move of the week."

"You weren't kidding about her teeth," says Caro.

"She refuses to get them fixed," I reply. "I don't know why."

Caro presses on her thigh, close to the site of her scar. Florence begins.

"The Flo-jitsu move I wanna show youse today, I call it the Kookaburra Laugh. It sounds like it's funny, but it isn't, 'specially for the person getting it." She grins, and a squirrel's squeak leaks out of her mouth. "I'm going to need a volunteer. A bad guy." She scans the room, and her search lands on me. "Come here, Munro."

All eyes laser-point my way. Caro nudges me forward.

"Um, okaaay." I shuffle to the front. Settling in beside Florence, I whisper, "You sure you don't want to thumb-wrestle instead?" She ignores me and addresses the class.

"So the Kookaburra Laugh is really good if you wanna get someone under control pretty quick. But you gotta be up close, within reach."

Without warning, her Swiss-cheese grin vanishes, replaced by the stony stare I've encountered on a regular basis. She spins me around and clamps onto my neck.

"The reason I call this the Kookaburra Laugh is 'cause it makes the bad guy giggle and cry at the same time."

The grip tightens, and it's like I'm being tickled with a pair of pliers. My eyes water. Giggles dribble from my lips. My knees start to give. I try to squirm away, but Florence just tightens her hold.

"You hear that? And can you see where I've got him?" She turns me with ease, deftly avoiding my flailing arms. "Make sure you get it right, where the neck and the shoulder muscles join together."

I'm going wobbly in the legs. It's like I just came out of the water at Centennial Beach on New Year's Day.

"Now, if your *sensei* kept goin', I could put Munro down on his knees, maybe even on the ground. Would you like to see that?"

There's a yes or two from the class. I want to shout no, but my throat is thinner than a drinking straw.

"I said, *would you like to see that?*"

A better response this time. They're going to be disappointed when I pass out.

"Well, as much as I would love to do it," says Florence, "I think this bad guy has had enough."

She releases me. I stagger away, moaning with relief. The class gives a round of applause. As they file out, Darrell reminds everyone not to practice on each other. I collapse into a nearby chair.

"Flo, don't I…get to try…on you?" I ask.

She cracks her knuckles. "Never."

Caro joins us. The two share intros and a few thoughts on self-defense. Caro lifts her shorts to reveal the scar on her leg.

"I could've done with a few of your moves when this happened," she says.

"But you got him, yeah?" asks Florence.

"How did you know it was a him?"

"It's always a him. And you got him, yeah?"

Caro's face goes rock hard for a second. "Yeah, I got him."

Florence grins. "Fuck yeah." She checks the time. "I gotta go. I wanna help Iggy stack shelves at the shop. But we can talk more this afternoon at the Shed." She looks at me and sighs. "I s'pose you'll be there too, Bad Guy."

"You're not doing another demo on me, are you?"

"If you didn't treat Ig so good, I would."

Florence departs. Caro lays her hands on my neck and begins massaging the site of the Kookaburra Laugh.

"You make a much better good guy," she says.

·············●···········

"Oh. My. GOD!"

Blake screams and hugs Caro. Then she hugs her again.

"Soooo pretty!" she says, punching me in the arm. "Just as well you're good-looking too, Munro! Otherwise, she would want a better boyfriend!"

"We're not together, Blake."

"What?"

"Caro isn't my girlfriend. We're not together."

Blake looks at Caro. She shrugs and nods. Blake looks at me like a disappointed coach. Before she can follow up with a comment, I redirect.

"Blake, why are you in this hut?"

"It's a gazebo."

"Okay, gazebo. Aren't you supposed to be doing agriculture this shift? Looks like a good time out there."

A girl whistles as she stacks mangoes into a wheelbarrow. A guy in a scruffy straw hat is down on his knees, talking softly to a bed of tomato plants. "Keep growing, babies…You're going well, babies…" A Working Partner is high-fiving a resident as the two of them bring a tractor back to the small barn.

"Agriculture Precinct is not my favorite. I hate getting dirty," says Blake. "So I do extra in the Digital Media Center."

"Are you working on something now?" asks Caro, nodding toward Blake's open laptop.

"This is something for me and Dale. Our wedding invitation."

"Oh, wow."

Blake spins the laptop around and pushes it across the table. "Could you look at it for me? My spelling is really bad."

Caro starts reading. I put a hand up to shield my eyes from the sun rays sneaking through the gaps in the gazebo. "Is Dale here? Does he hate getting dirty too?"

Blake busts out one of her giant laughs. "No chance! Agriculture Precinct is *totally* his favorite! He stinks like hell when he's finished a shift."

"What about Shah? He's scheduled to be here too, yeah?"

"I haven't seen him today. I think he chucked a sickie."

"Uh-huh."

Caro raises a thumb. "This is great, Blake. I love the border of roses. Only two spelling mistakes that I could see: *occasion* has just the one *s* and *celebration* has a second *e* instead of an *a*."

Blake punches me in the arm again. "Pretty *and* smart."

"Oh, and you didn't put in a date," Caro says.

Blake flicks her hair. "That's right."

"You haven't decided on a date yet?"

"No, there isn't one." She delivers the spiel I've heard several times now, about how her dad won't allow her and Dale to get married. Caro fidgets and frowns. She's about to launch into a response when Dale rocks up to the gazebo, all grime and sweat and a grin to put the Joker to shame. Blake stiff-arms his cheeky attempt at a hug and lifts his iPad from her bulging handbag. He taps the screen and bows in Caro's direction.

Hey, I'm Dale.

"I'm Caro."

More taps. **Would you like a tour of the Agriculture Precinct?**

"Well, we're here to help, Dale," I say. "We did enough touring during the school term, eh?"

He makes a sound, a cross between a cough and a "meh."

We've done the tasks for today. Watering, spraying, bringing stuff to the kitchens. Tomorrow there is more to do.

I clap my hands, hoping it hides my disappointment. "I guess a bit more touring wouldn't hurt."

Dale fist-bumps Caro and me, blows a kiss to Blake, then leads the way. He takes us through the greenhouse and the barn and the vegetable patches. He gives us the lowdown on Fair Go's produce, with a special mention for basil. **It goes good in hot, dry weather. Too good. We have so much bloody pesto to sell!**

Dale then escorts us a short distance along the fence line that separates the property from "the Bush." He says the neighboring forest reserve is the biggest in Brisbane and is mostly made up of eucalyptus trees. It's home to more than a hundred different types of wildlife, including wallabies, koalas, echidnas and powerful owls. As I digest Dale's info, it occurs to me I've never felt bad before that he can't speak. A chunk of me feels it today though. The voice program's burry monotone and occasional half-assed pronunciations don't come close to conveying the passion in his gestures and facial expressions.

We head back, passing by the herb gardens and a big mango tree that has an abandoned bathtub beside it. On the path to the gazebo, Dale picks an orange flower from one of the garden beds. He hands it to Blake on bended knee.

"This smells better than you," she says.

Dale rolls his eyes, then waves at Caro and me. **I'll see you soon, after I've had a shower.**

We leave the Agriculture Precinct. Before we're out of range, we hear Blake's final, shouted command. "You should make her your girlfriend, Munro! Then take her back to Canada, Munro!"

·············●···········

Around three, we roll up to the Shed, Fair Go's indoor basketball court. Kelvin is there. My team as well, minus Shah.

"So what's the big secret, guys?" I ask. "You got a Zamboni here or something?"

"What is a Zamboni?" asks Bernie. "Is that a type of pasta?"

"I think it's one of Infecto's archenemies," suggests Iggy.

"Good guesses. It's actually kind of like a lawn mower that makes the ice nice and smooth on a rink," says Kelvin, creating more confusion. "No, Munro, we couldn't get you a Zamboni. But we don't need one for floor hockey, do we?"

Dale emerges from a storage locker with two large equipment bags. He follows it up by dragging out a full six-by-four net and setting it up on the nearest baseline.

"The blue bag next to Florence's feet—that's probably the one you want to check out," says Kelvin.

I walk over, kneel down beside the stacked Bauer bag, pull back the zip. "You bought goalie gear?"

"We did, yeah."

"For me."

"Technically, it's for the residents, but who else has a clue what to do with it?"

I take the pieces out and lay them in a semicircle around me, just as I would on game day. Caro kneels beside me. "What's that thing?" she asks, pointing.

"That's a blocker. Goes on this hand."

She nods. "Your right? Makes sense."

The final item in the bag is the helmet. I hold it up and out, like I'm Hamlet with his skull. It's literally a work of art. The lump in my throat gets bigger, heavier.

"Who painted this?"

"We all did," says Blake. "I painted the heart inside the maple leaf. Ig did the Brisbane Wheel. Bernie wrote *Freetard*, of course. Flo did the weird three-leg sign—"

"I wanted to do a middle finger," she says. "But Iggy said I shouldn't. So I did this—a *mitsu-tomoe*. It's a symbol *samurai* families had in Japan."

"Whatever," Blake says. "Dale did the wattle tree. And Kelvin painted the zombie wombat."

"It's a squirrel, Blake," corrects Kelvin.

"A zombie squirrel."

My fingers brush over the glossy surface, absorbing the awesome artwork. They stop on a small pic under the right ear hole. A black pawn. "I wonder who did this one?"

"Me."

Shah ambles in from the entrance. He's wearing a Lionel Messi Barcelona team shirt that's one, maybe two, sizes too big for him. There's a couple of extra lines on his face. My guess is they're from the cushions on his couch.

"I am tired of beating you in checkers," he says.

"You're tired of beating me? I don't think so. I think you're tired of *getting* beat."

"Yeah?"

"Yeah!"

"You think?"

"I think!"

We eyeball each other for a second, all puffed chests and fake sneers. Then we crack up, me laughing, Shah twitching his lips. The truth of our checkess games over the past month is we've both been winning. Little by little, Shah's using more chess moves, usually without warning, occasionally with a half smile. If only YOLO could be there with a camera to make it all legit. They could call the video *Checkmates For Life*.

Kelvin unzips the second Bauer bag and starts passing sticks around. "So I think we've done enough dillydallying. Time to get this show on the road." He picks up a ball and rolls his arm over, a la cricket bowling. "We could use your help, Munro."

I stand and scan the group. These faces. Looking at me. Looking *to* me.

I don't feel so much like a Living Partner right now. I feel like something more, something close to family. A brother, maybe.

A big brother.

....••••••●••••••••...

We did basic stickhandling stuff, Evie. Like when I was in seventh grade and we did floor hockey with your class. Keep Away. Red Light/Green Light. Then a couple of passing drills, one in pairs going up and down the floor and another one, Around the House. You remember that? Everyone gets in a circle and does random passes. So fun! Then we did a shootout to finish. I dressed in the goalie gear and faced some fire from the team. Except for Kelvin, I made sure everyone scored a goal, even Shah, who didn't want a stick. He kicked the ball instead.

I wish you'd been there to see it.

"Are you talking to me, Munro Maddux?"

Caro's brief doze is over. Her head, though, still rests against the train window.

"No. Just myself."

"Where are we?"

I look out the window, squinting into the setting sun. Stretches of golf course glide by. A group of men in plaid shorts hacks at the long grass beside the tracks while a pair of crows keeps watch over their cart. "About ten minutes to Wattle Ridge."

"I'll go back to my nap then."

"More sleep? I'm going to start calling you Shah."

"Been a big day."

"Been a great day."

Caro rubs her nose, pulls her hat down lower. "Hey, at the end of First Aid with that fella Perry, what did he want to talk to you about?"

"Nothing much." I plant an elbow on the window frame and rest my head on my open hand. "He wanted to make sure I didn't feel uncomfortable in the class."

Caro shifts. I see her puzzled reflection in the window. "Was there a reason for you to feel uncomfortable?"

"None whatsoever."

"You sure?"

"Totally."

"I remember you spaced out a bit at the start."

"That was just your bad hygiene. Look, let's change the subject, eh? There's so much awesomeness from today we should focus on instead."

She nods. "Yeah, we should. Although I felt sad for Blake with that wedding invitation. I'd love to give her father a gobful."

"*That's* your change of subject?"

"Sorry. It's the future lawyer in me. If someone's copping a bad deal, I want to defend them, I want to make things better for them. It's what I do."

"What you do, Caro, is sleep on the train. So how about you do some more of it. I'll wake you up when we're getting close."

To my surprise, she heeds my advice. She brings her legs up onto the seat, leans against the window and crashes before the next station, her whistly nose-breathing a dead giveaway she's out. I resist the urge to lean across and sneak a kiss on her slightly parted lips. Instead, I close my eyes. The wires thrum above my head. The wheels gallop under my feet.

Make things better.

For them.

From day one, the student exchange was about regaining myself and getting rid of the Coyote. Now that I'm within reach of that goal, I can look beyond it. Who do I want to be? What do I want to do?

I have an idea. A big idea. One that means I won't just be leaving the past here.

..............●..............

Mom and Dad:

Things are great. Best they've been since I arrived. Best since Evie died, to tell the truth.

Hey, what would you think of the Foundation setting up an assisted-living residence like Fair Go back home? Would it be possible? Would you be interested? I know it would involve a ton of cash and time and godknowswhatelse, but I think it would be awesome.

Just a thought for the future.

Talk soon.
M

THE JAIL

Fifty hours.

Today's Straya Tour trip will see that number officially reached. April 17, first weekend of term two. It's been a snap of the fingers. It's been a lifetime. A life-*changing* time. Just like it promised.

The Coyote's gone, but I won't forget the place that muzzled it. I'll keep doing Wednesday afternoons until Shah plays a full game of chess. For the rest of the exchange, I'll come back every now and then, to listen and talk and guide. Hang out. Play some floor hockey.

I'm sad my volunteer time is up, but I'm also stoked for today. Shah shared some exciting news at the end of last Wednesday's visit.

I am taking my turn this week on tour. I am choosing place to go, he said.

Finally! A fitting end to the fifty for sure. I'd tried my best to bait the place out of him, but he wouldn't bite.

You will find out soon enough, he said, waving goodbye from his front door.

························●···········

"Can I have a word?"

"Sure."

Kelvin pulls me aside in front of the bus.

"Whassup?" I say, flicking a dead bug from the grille. Kelvin removes his sunglasses and hangs them off his shirt collar. His face has more sheen than usual, and there's a thin line of sweat across his top lip. I don't think I've seen Kelvin Yow sweat before, not even on the hot-as-hell days.

"Shah's not here," he says.

"He's late?"

"No."

"He bailed on his turn?"

"No. He's not here." Kelvin scuffs at the asphalt with his sneaker. "He left, Munro. Cleared out of Fair Go. I don't think he'll be coming back."

"What are you talking about? I just saw him on Wednesday. He played like, ten checkers moves the entire game. Everything else was chess." I look up into the front seats of the bus, expecting to see laughing "gotcha" faces. "Is this for the video? Are you punking me?"

Kelvin shakes his head. "He left Thursday, mate. He made the decision to cut ties and go back to a family of Afghani refugees in Goodna. He lived with them when he first got to Brisbane, but they couldn't give him the specialized assistance he needed, so that's how he came to be with us. Now, it appears circumstances have changed." He drops a hand on my shoulder. "I'm sorry, Munro. I know you and him had a good thing going."

Found you.

I'm reeling. The air has left my lungs. I suddenly have my sister's tongue, too big for my mouth, making it tough for words to form and find their way out. A brisk wind skips through the parking lot, carrying twigs, brown leaves, an empty coffee cup. And invisible knives aimed at my right hand. I scrunch my eyes tight, willing a loophole to appear.

"It *appears* circumstances have changed…that's what you said?"

"Yes."

"So you just…let him go?"

"No. In our discussions, I stated a number of times that I felt Shah's best placement was here. But ultimately, the decision to stay or go can only be made by the residents themselves and their custodial connections. Shah and the Goodna family made their decision, and we have to respect that."

No we don't! I silently shout. What if it's the wrong decision? I get the whole shared culture thing, but it's not like this is Shah's actual family. Is he going to sleep less with them? Do more? And what about the chess? For fuck's sake, he's almost there! Who's going to take him those final few steps?

Not you, Munro Maddux.

"I must've done something wrong."

"You didn't."

"Why didn't he just ask for a different Living Partner? At least then he'd still be around."

"There's nothing more you could have done, mate. He's not gone because of you. Things just happen. My old man has a saying: 'Sometimes, Life takes on a life of its own.'" He digs into the side pocket of his cargo shorts and extracts a small object. A black pawn. "Shah asked me to give you this. He said he enjoyed kicking your arse."

I stand the piece on my open palm. After a few seconds it tips, and I have to grab for it so it doesn't fall to the ground.

"Did he leave an address?" I ask. "Email, phone, anything?"

"No."

The bus horn bleats. Bernie, dressed in a Helvetica Freetard shirt, is in the driver's seat. She points to her watch and pretends to turn the steering wheel. Kelvin nods and waves.

"We should go." Kelvin shifts his head to one side, peers at me through narrowed eyes. "You okay to do this?"

I stuff the pawn in my shirt pocket. My heart thumps against it.

"I gotta finish my fifty hours."

Kelvin half smiles, makes for the driver's-side door, stops. "By the way, the guys wanted to dedicate the tour trip today to Shah, so we're still going to the place he chose before leaving."

"What did he choose?"

Kelvin puts his sunglasses back on. "Boggo Road. It's a jail."

There's nothing more you could have done.

That's a lie, isn't it, Munro?

People say that when you try to stop something bad from happening and then it happens anyway. It was all you heard after Evie died. From family, friends, strangers. The doctor at the hospital who pronounced her dead. Your mom and dad said the words too, but they knew.

There is always more you could've done. Made one more phone call, driven one more mile, asked one more question, read one more book. Held on for one more second. You can tell yourself you did your best, and it may even be true; you might be able to say it with a straight face and sleep like the dead that night. But your best is never the best. That's a fact. And in the end, your less than best has only one measure: Did the bad thing happen?

You should have done more.

I can't sit still. My left hand is clamped on my head. My right—I've wrapped it in my shirt. It looks like I broke it and put together a makeshift sling. The team is wondering what's going on. Bernie is blinking. Blake and Dale take turns glancing over from across the aisle. Iggy's tracking me rather than the car on our tail. Even Florence is a little off balance.

Get it together, Munro. Count your breaths. Ten? Better make it twenty.

The Coyote's not back.

Not for real.

This is a hiccup, a stumbling block. An echo. That's all. I got blindsided. Yes, Shah's gone, but the others are still here. I still have them. And they're the key. It doesn't matter that my time is up. I can be there for them. I can do more for them.

The Coyote's not back.

No way.

·············●●·············

We arrive at the Boggo Road Gaol. Our tour guide walks us through all the modern services they provide—film shoots, parties, weddings, corporate retreats. A marquee has been set up in the main courtyard, with a podium and chairs and white flowers all around. I recognize the opportunity immediately. I lay it out for Kelvin.

"Say what?" he says.

I go through it again.

"You're serious."

"What do you guys say…deadset?"

Kelvin frowns, puts his hands on his hips. "I don't know. It's actually a pretty cool idea, but I don't know."

"It's not for real, obviously," I add. "But I think it would mean a whole lot to them." I point to the small stage area of the marquee. "Check it out! It's like they put this together just for us! We have to do this!"

Kelvin looks me up and down and whistles. "Check *you* out. You're certainly fired up. Where's this coming from? Is it because of Shah? You think you have to make up for that somehow?"

"No."

"I'll say it again, mate. It wasn't your fault. You shouldn't feel bad."

"This isn't about what happened earlier, Kelvin. This isn't about feeling bad. This is about *doing good*."

You don't give a crap about them.

This is all about you.

"These guys can have the moment they've dreamed about, a moment they deserve. Right here, right now."

Kelvin considers the team, spread throughout the courtyard. They're swinging on the gates, pointing at the tower, surrendering to finger guns. Iggy mentions to Florence that he feels safe—a bad guy wouldn't dare follow us here. Bernie says Shah would've liked learning about the riot that happened in 1988.

"You know what the deal is, don't you?" says Kelvin.

"I do. Blake and Dale have to agree to it."

"That's right. And if they're good, this stays in the group. Everyone has to understand that. Photos have to be on Blake's and Dale's devices, no one else's. No video, and that includes yours truly. This is private, not for sharing on social media."

"Agree totally."

Kelvin smiles and snaps his fingers. "Well, what are you waiting for? Go find out if we're having a wedding today."

Bernie blinks several times, then opens her hands.

"Okay, we don't have long. I've never done this before, but I've seen lots of movies." She claps once, then commences. "Dearly beloved, we are gathered here today at this prison to celebrate the pretend marriage of Blake and Dale. If anyone knows why these two lovebirds should not be joined in pretend marriage, speak now or forever shut your gob."

The "wedding party"—best man Iggy, brides-maid Florence and the happy couple—looks toward the assembled audience of Kelvin, me and the Boggo Road Gaol tour guide.

"We're good," I say, giving a thumbs-up.

Bernie rolls her shoulders. "Okay. So I know the two of you have had wedding vows prepared for ages, in case you ever had the chance to say them. Well, here we are. Blake, would you like to start?"

Blake takes the iPad from the groom's hands. She fills her lungs, exhales and waves a hand in front of her eyes, warding off the tears.

"Dale, I take you to be my guy, to hug and to kiss on this day and all the other days after that. I promise not to laugh too loud, or complain too much when you watch *Totally Wild* on TV, or sneak swearwords into your voice program. I promise to listen to you and respect you and support you and love you. Most of all, I promise to live as your girl, now and forever."

With a broad grin, Blake gives the iPad back. Florence hands over a crumpled tissue, and Blake dabs away the tear tracks on her red, round cheeks.

"Your turn, big fella," says Bernie.

Dale takes the hand of his bride and kisses it. He opens the voice program.

Blake, I take you to be my girl, to hug and to kiss on this day and all the other days after that. I promise not to hide your 'furreal friends,' or burn your French toast, or stink you out after a long day sweating in the sun. I promise to listen to you and respect you and support you and love you. Most of all, I promise to live as your guy, now and forever.

"Ignatius?" asks Bernie. "Do you have the Fruit Tingles?"

Iggy lifts the candy from his pocket, two pieces. He hands them to the couple with a Fabergé-egg level of care.

"Good thing you had those," I say to Kelvin.

He shrugs. "Life Savers would've been better."

"Blake, do you take this guy to be your guy?"

"I do."

She places the candy on Dale's open palm. He lifts it to his open mouth and drops it in.

"Dale, do you take this girl to be your girl?"

I do.

He returns the Tingle favor. Bernie nods.

"By the power vested in me as creator of the Freetard line of clothing—shirts $19.99, caps $14.99—I now pronounce you together forever. You may kiss each other. But no tongues, please. And no exchanging Fruit Tingles. That's gross."

Dale and Blake lock lips. Iggy applauds. Florence does a celebratory Flo-jitsu move. The iPad approves with a pre-programmed, **AWWW, YEAH!**

After the photos—two each on the newlyweds' devices—Blake runs over and throws her arms around my neck.

"Thank you, Munro!" she says in my ear, her voice way too loud. "That was the best moment of my life!"

I pat her back. "So stoked for you and Dale."

She separates, squeals and returns to her "husband." He's staring at the photos, mist gathering in his eyes. The wedding party soon morphs back into a tour group and follows the guide toward the cell blocks. Kelvin and I bring up the rear.

"I've seen plenty of Fair Go moments in my time. Not too many better than that," he says. "How do you feel?"

I take the black pawn out of my shirt pocket and toss it from hand to hand. My face is achy from smiling so much. My head is clear.

"I feel like I did good."

Kelvin nods. "Can't argue with that, Munro. Can't argue with that at all."

..........●●●..........

I should be dog-tired, dozing, destined for some faraway platform on the opposite side of Brisbane. I'm not tired. I'm wide awake. That's what a wake-up call will do.

The school planner is out of my bag. The calendar is open. In my hand is a red marker. It looms over the grid of dates, ready to strike.

The first X—*Vaccination Day*—is marked as the train leaves Banfield station. There are six more *X*s by the time the announcement for Wattle Ridge comes over the PA.

"Rowan's gonna be real busy deleting messages," I murmur.

..........●●●..........

"So how was it? Where did your mate Shah choose, Munro?"

"Boggo Road Gaol."

Geordie and Nina exchange a glance across the dinner table. Rowan says, "Awesome" through a mouthful of his incredible bacon-potato pie.

"Brings back some memories," replies Geordie, between glugs of his XXXX beer. "How'd it go?"

"Bad start, but it got better."

"Did Shah enjoy it?"

I set my knife and fork down on the plate. "That was the bad start. He wasn't there. He left Fair Go last Thursday. Gone for good."

"Oh, I'm so sorry, Mun," says Nina, levering another slice of pie out of the pan. "From what you told us, you did a lot of good for him."

"It wasn't enough. But I won't make that mistake again."

The Hydes' faces turn wary, each of the trio silently chewing on my vow. Nina wipes away a dot of grease from the table. Geordie splashes Worcestershire sauce on the last of his vegetables. Rowan studies a slightly over-cooked scrap of bacon. A long minute passes; the sounds of supper fade. I kill the pause, compliment "MasterChef Rowan," gather up the Hydes' empty dinner plates and, with my own still half filled, carry all four to the kitchen. After dumping my leftovers in the garbage and depositing the plates in the dishwasher, I return to the table.

"If it's okay, I'd like to be excused."

"You mean from the table or from the mistake you made?"

Geordie makes out like he's joking, but there's a kernel of something underneath. Frustration? Disappointment?

"You're excused, mate," he adds before I can figure out what to say. "Catch you later? Row and I are gonna watch a tape of the Broncs game from this arvo."

"Absolutely."

I start to step away.

"Munro?"

"Yeah?

"One last thing."

"Okay."

Geordie delivers his words like they're written on palm cards. "Your heart is in the right place. That's been clear from the beginning when you told us about Mr. Adams and how he tried to save your sister. You said you're searching for his spirit?"

"I am."

Geordie stands and brings a hand to his barrel chest. His mouth twitches, as if there's voltage in the words he's about to say.

"Are you sure it's *his* spirit you're looking for?"

He sees you, Munro.

On your knees, keeping Evie's head still. Working on her. Chest compressions, breaths. Keeping going, not stopping. Not stopping when it was all too late.

It was you that held her hand. It was you that let go.

He knows, Munro.

He knows it was you.

··········●●···········

Before the rugby match replay, I invite Rowan to hang out for a bit in my room. I tell him about all the Fair Go time I mean to do this term. He walks to the corner nearest the window, grabs the little stuffed koala clinging to the stem of the pedestal fan and attaches it to his middle finger.

"I take that to mean you won't be wiping any more phone calls."

"You gotta help me out here, man," he says. "You gotta give me a reason."

"I thought you said you would keep doing it. That it was like littering for you."

"It is."

"You said you wanted to help me."

Rowan pats the koala on the head. "I am helping you, brother. And I will keep helping you. But you gotta get real now, Mun. You gotta talk about what happened."

I tilt my head, allowing my hair to fall forward. I look at Rowan through the dark curtain. "You still don't know?"

"No."

"You didn't look it up out of curiosity?"

He smiles. "No. Didn't search any of the million articles out there."

"More like ten."

"A million, ten…not cool either way."

"What about your dad?"

"What about him?"

"He didn't look it up?"

"He's not much of a Googler."

"At supper, it just seemed like he…knew."

Rowan sits in the office chair. "He doesn't know about you, but he knows what's going on. He sees you."

I move so I'm seated on the edge of the bed, my legs dangling over the side. My heels bounce against the wooden frame.

"It goes no further than this room."

"Only if you say otherwise."

The story I told in the Thai restaurant my first week—I tell the same one now, only Mr. Adams is nowhere to be found. Where was Evie's favorite teacher when she lay dying in the corridor between the library and Mrs. Bouchard's class? Probably on the other side of the Pacific Ocean, back in his hometown of Brisbane. Certainly thousands of miles from DSS. I wonder if he even knows what happened. I wonder if he's even aware that his brightest star fell from the sky.

Rowan listens without reaction. No *What the?* or *I can't even* or *That's totally messed up.* At the finish, he strokes the peach fuzz on his top lip, crosses his legs, leans on one of the office chair's armrests.

"You need a drink of water?"

"I'm okay."

He closes one eye. "Bundy and Coke?"

"Pass."

"How's it feel to unload that stuff?"

I count out three breaths, then answer, "Makes me want to jump on a train and head back to Fair Go."

Rowan nods and gets to his feet. He tosses the koala to me and shoves his hands deep into his jeans pockets.

"I'll rub out as many messages as I can."

As he heads for the door, he has the last word. "The residents out there—they're not your sister, man. And they're not your chance to make things right."

•••••••••●•••••••••

I sit the koala on my bedside table. He looks a bit lost, his outstretched arms pleading for something to hang on to.

"I gotcha, buddy."

I dig into my shirt pocket and pull out the black pawn. It's a perfect fit.

I do fifty push-ups, then get into bed and turn out the light.

So, you gave me a scare today, Coyote. A little throwback to the bad old days.

It's done though. The Fair Go effect is about to go into overdrive. No more scares, no more glitches, no more echoes. Just goodbye. For good. It's the home stretch, Coyote. Starting tomorrow.

Sleep well tonight.

You too, Munro.

Just like Shah.

HOME

"I'm sorry…what exactly are you saying?"

Craig Varzani pulls his shoulders back. The red poppy on his lapel (WTF, dude—ANZAC Day was two weeks ago) dips and bobs, as if trying to avoid eye contact. For the fourth time since taking a seat in Ms. Mac's office, he reads from the notepad in his lap.

"In the last few days, Munro, I've become aware of the full details surrounding your student exchange to date. Your marks are average at best, and you're not actively engaging in school life or participating in extra-curricular activities. These were points of discussion at our previous check-in meeting, and there hasn't been any improvement since then. While these would be concerning on their own, additional matters brought to my attention have escalated the situation considerably. I've been reliably informed that there have been other issues, including altercations with students."

I glare at Ms. MacGillivray. She doesn't look up, preferring to focus on the paper in her hands.

"They were early in first term," I say. "There hasn't been an issue for over two months."

Varzani tweaks his bumblebee-colored glasses. "That's true. But it appears you replaced the fighting with something else—truancy. You've missed an unacceptable amount of school recently, Munro."

"So what you're saying is, I'm no longer da man. Is that what you're telling me?"

Varzani ignores my sass. "This is not the sort of behavior we want associated with YOLO." He takes off his glasses. "I rang your parents this morning and informed them of the situation. I recommended that you go home."

"Home?"

"Yes."

"No warning? No second chance?"

"This was your second chance."

I shake my head. "My parents won't agree."

"I wouldn't be so sure about that. They felt you should go home too. But they wanted to tell you in person." He checks his fluor-yellow fitness band. "That was almost two hours ago."

I feel for the phone in my shorts pocket. In this brief lull, I half expect FaceTime to fire up and burn a hole right through to my skin. It stays quiet, though, the way it has been all morning. The only notification I've received so far was a text from Caro, **thinking of you** and a series of emojis: kissy-face, sad face, love heart, broken heart. She couldn't know about this, could she?

"This is BS. I don't get a vote?"

"In all fairness, Munro, you had a vote. You agreed to the terms of the exchange; you read the rules; you knew the expectations."

"Look, I didn't ditch anything that mattered, did I? The Thirty-Hour Famine? The Athletics Carnival? Vaccination Day? Really? And I wasn't truly *ditching*! You know where I was."

Varzani unbuttons his jacket. The ANZAC poppy stares at the door. "Your commitment to Fair Go— it's admirable, no question. But here's the thing. Once your fifty hours were up, continuing to go there had nothing to do with *school*. And that's regrettable, Munro. It really is. Because this is a *school* exchange program. Your folks paid us a lot of money so you could come to Australia for *school*." He closes his notepad. "You are a decent young man. And you've been through hell. If Fair Go is your calling, maybe you should come back."

"Come back?"

"Yes. Maybe in a couple of years, on a temporary visa. Or you could work in a care-facility type of setup when you return home."

I turn to Ms. Mac. "Help me out here. Please."

She cricks her neck and leans forward, elbows on her knees. Traces of a black eye are visible under her makeup. "I'm sorry, Munro. It's too late for me to help. When you get back to Vancouver, you should definitely get in touch with...what was the name of that counselor your mum mentioned in her email?"

"Ollie."

"Ollie. You and she can work on a plan that will find your best and doesn't involve sacrificing your education."

I let the words percolate in my head. Then I stand and extend a hand to Ms. Mac.

"You're leaving?" she says.

"Yeah. I've got a lot less time than I thought I had. You'd think I would've learned that by now." I turn to Varzani. "You know where I'll be."

"Come on, Munro, my man. You're not a criminal. And this doesn't have to be a difficult exit."

I walk toward the door of Ms. Mac's office.

"Craig, my man...too late."

························●···········

I'm sick to my stomach. This can't be happening, not when the finish line of my recovery is so close. I can't say goodbye yet. I'm not ready.

My feet move quickly, walking fast, then jogging. They work in isolation from the rest of my body, as if someone's controlling them with a remote. Past classrooms, along corridors, up stairs. I'm headed for my locker. But that fact is in the distance, somewhere on the horizon. A single thought is taking up all the available space in my head:

I'm headed home.

You knew this would happen, Munro.

Deep down in your heart, you knew.

You can be away from me for an hour, a day. Even a few weeks. But it could never be permanent. You could never leave me here. You need me too much.

Munro and the Coyote—we are together.

Forever.

I fumble with the key, then try to insert it upside down. Swearwords are muttered. My hands steady. I flip the door open, and it crashes against Toby Gresham's locker with its peeling Pantera sticker. My bag and the folders of my Fair Go team—stained and bent from so much handling—are the only things I need. Planner, textbooks, spare school shirt…no longer required.

"Munro?"

Caro is standing in the middle of the hallway.

"I know what happened. I'm…I'm totally gutted for you."

I'm set to ask how she found out about my take-down, but the question fizzles. Caro's face is *nuit*.

She's been crying, Munro. And it's not because you're going home, Munro.

She knows.

I point a shaky finger at her. "Rowan told you, didn't he?"

"Rowan?"

"About Evie. He fucking told you."

"No. He didn't."

"Why would he do that?"

"Munro—"

"He promised to stay quiet. He's a fucking liar."

"Rowan didn't say a thing." Caro steps forward. She holds a hand up toward me like I'm a dangerous dog. "I found out off my own bat. You were bailing on school so much, I was worried things were getting worse for you."

Her palms come together and push up under her trembling chin.

"I spoke with Ms. Mac. I told her I was concerned. She didn't want to say anything, but I got a tiny bit of info out of her, enough that I did a search on your old school. I found the article about…about what happened."

My phone starts to buzz. FaceTime. I block the call.

"I'm here for you."

Caro searches her pockets, finds a folded piece of paper. She opens it and passes it to me. I stare at the creased page. It's a poster. The content—pics, logo, colors—I know very well. A familiar button sits in the center.

Sussex State High—support our exchange student, Munro Maddux!

Munro's sister, Evelyn, passed away at age 13, and the The Evelyn Maddux Foundation was established in her honor.

Buy an E-LIFE badge for $2 and fund Down syndrome awareness and research!

They all know.

It's just as well we're going home.

"Don't worry," says Caro. "It's just a draft. It hasn't gone out anywhere. I got the go-ahead from student council, and I got in touch with your folks about the buttons. They're on the way. Could definitely sell a ton of them this term."

She takes hold of my left hand. Her wet cheeks shine in the hallway light.

"What happened to you, Munro, losing your sister like that—I can't imagine how that feels. And I can't blame you for seeing school as a shit place to be. But for the rest of the exchange"—she nods toward the poster—"I hope this helps you stick around a bit more."

Ha! Not gonna happen.

My hand slides out of Caro's grasp. I tear the poster in half, put it in my locker, close the door. The look on Caro's face is shifting by the second, through shock, then alarm, then something close to outright panic.

"The exchange is done," I say. "I fucked up. YOLO contacted my parents—they're calling it quits. I guess I'll be on a plane tomorrow or the next day. Either way, I'm headed home."

Caro hugs herself, arms crossed over the sternum, hands clasped to her shoulders, knuckles white. Her black fingernails and wristbands are like fresh bruises. Her scattered hair hides much of her bowed face.

"So…this is goodbye?" she asks.

Not the voice you wanted saying those words, eh?

"I'm sorry," I say.

A shudder rolls over her. "I could come to Fair Go with you. That's where you're going now, isn't it? I could ditch, and we could go together one last time."

"Ditching is not what you do, Caro."

In my pocket FaceTime buzzes for the second time. Again I kill the call. The school bell rings. Last class is starting. The drone of students roaming from one class to the next begins to die away.

"It wasn't supposed to end like this, Munro. Not today. Not this way."

"I know. I'm sorry."

I open my arms. She falls in, buries her breaking face in my shoulder. Two minutes pass, a poor substitute for what's left of six months. I take everything in. The curve of her back, the coconut smell of her hair, the squeak of her small sobs. The punch of her hammering heart. It's the best I can do.

"I'll text you."

Caro wipes her eyes with my shirt sleeve. "Don't."

"Okay."

We break apart. Caro takes hold of my left hand again, squeezes it, lets it fall back to my side.

"Say hi to the team for me."

She turns and runs away, headed for H Block.

·········●●··········

Varzani said I'm not a criminal, but maybe I am. Maybe I'm a fugitive. The Coyote always accused me of hiding out in Fair Go. Maybe I could do just that. Lie low there for a while, refuse to turn myself in. Seriously, what the fuck could **YOLO** do about it? Call the cops? Arrest me? Put me in handcuffs and force me to leave?

I could convince Kelvin to keep me around. I could do other stuff, not just be a Living Partner. I have some money. I could stay in the staff units. They have a spare room or two.

This is not over.

This is not goodbye.

·········•●•··········

I knock on the door to Kelvin's office. The muffled murmurs inside continue for several seconds before I hear a strained "Who is it?"

"It's Munro Maddux."

Silence, then more muffled murmurs. "Get on with it," I whisper. Time is short. And getting shorter. Finally, there's a "Come in." I enter to find Kelvin on his cell.

"I know where you're coming from, no doubt... That's right...Okay, I'll be in touch. Bye." He puts down the phone and looks me over like I'm a piece of abstract art.

"Munro Maddux. The young man I need to talk to, and *poof!* You appear just like that. I would say you're psychic, but I don't think you're aware of our recent situation."

"I don't know about any situation. What's up?"

"First things first. Why are you wagging school to come here?"

"Sorry?"

Kelvin folds his arms. "You can only do so many 'diversity projects' before the truth is apparent. What's going on, mate? Why did you bail on school to come here today?"

It's all falling apart, Munro.

I wince, nod. "You're right, Kelvin, I've been ditching. But it's actually not the case this time. I'm here because I want to...stay."

Kelvin's eyes narrow. He begins drumming his fingers on the mouse pad to his right. "Stay. You mean...*live*?"

"Yes. In the staff units, if you have room."

"How long were you hoping to stay?"

"As long as you'll have me."

"Your host family been a problem?"

"No. They're not the problem."

Kelvin stops drumming. "Do the student-exchange people know about this? They can't be okay with you making this request."

"There is no student exchange. It ended this morning. So did my Sussex State High stint. I'm not ditching now. I'm a free man."

"Free?"

"Free to be here at Fair Go."

"Okay, but if the exchange is over, won't you be on your way back to Vancouver soon?"

"I'm not ready to say goodbye."

Kelvin leans back in his chair, plants his hands on top of his head. He starts a comment, but it falters in transit, peters out to a soft *hmmm*. He stands up and begins a lap of the office. One by one, he finds the framed pics of him with my team. Florence mid-arm wrestle. Iggy pointing at a vine of big ripe tomatoes. Bernie talking into a microphone. Dale going full farmer with overalls, boots, straw hat. Kelvin returns to the desk and opens one of the drawers. He takes out an unframed pic and lays it face down.

"The photos on display," he says, "they're the residents who currently call this place home. I make sure I get a snap with each person, print off a copy and frame it. I love seeing them and being around them every day."

He points at the open drawer.

"I also keep photos in my desk. These are the folks that used to live here at one time or another, but now they're gone."

He turns over the pic. It's Shah, in his Barcelona shirt, arms folded, right foot propped on top of a soccer ball.

"I would love to keep these photos on show too, but I don't. Putting them away reminds me that things don't stay the same, that people leave. That we walk side by side with our residents rather than holding their hands."

A thought hits me. I scan the office gallery once, twice, then zone back in on the residential manager.

"Where's Blake?"

The color leaches out of Kelvin's face. He reaches into the drawer, finds a photo and places it face up next to Shah's. Blake is eating ice cream and rocking the peace sign.

"Early Monday," he begins, "Tom Kennedy came across one of the 'wedding' pics from Boggo Road on his daughter's phone. He was livid and rang me immediately, demanding an explanation. I assured him that the ceremony was nothing more than spur-of-the-moment, harmless fun, that it had no actual meaning, no formal recognition. It was simply a wonderful moment of affection and commitment between two loving people. He saw it very differently. *Blake has Down syndrome. She's handicapped. She can't properly grasp affection and commitment. She has no real clue about relationships. She sees marriage as some sort of fairy tale, not what it truly is: a holy union between a man and a woman of sound mind, sanctioned by God.* Tom said we'd been grossly irresponsible and had gone against his express wishes. We'd indulged his daughter's unrealistic expectations and he would forever have to deal with the fallout. Shame on us. He wanted to know whose idea it was. I said it was mine. He wondered what sort of sadistic organization we were running and mentioned he was considering legal action. In the meantime, he was taking Blake out of Fair Go, effective immediately.

"I apologized unreservedly and asked him how I could make things right. Anything short of turning back time was unacceptable. I asked him—no, not asked, *begged* him—to not have Blake pay the price for a mistake that we made. I pleaded with him to consider her work in the Digital Media Center and the pride and sense of achievement and responsibility and self-worth she'd gotten from it. Should all that be swept aside because of a momentary miscalculation? I said straight up that Fair Go is Blake's *home*. Tom Kennedy laughed and said, *Some sort of home.* He reckoned we'd get Blake and *that boy* living together and sleeping in the same bed. Before long, he'd have *a retarded grandchild to look after.*

"Next morning, he collected Blake and her belongings. I won't share the details of that scene with you, Munro. Suffice to say it was tense. And awful. And sad."

Kelvin rises, walks around his desk and grabs a spare chair. He sets it down directly in front of me and sits. We are face to face, knee to knee.

"You're blaming yourself," he says. "But sometimes, Life takes on a life of its own. Fair Go is not immune to that truth. It's why we walk side by side. It's why I keep those pictures in my desk drawer."

He leans forward and pats my shin.

"It's why you should think about going home, Munro."

My phone comes alive again, bustling and vibrating. I take it out and shut it off. It goes back in my pocket. Silent. Dead.

I stand up, sling my bag over my shoulder and walk out of Kelvin's office.

She's gone.

Taken away.

Stolen.

You tried to do more, tried to do good. Be the big brother she could be proud of. But you let her down. You failed.

Now you'll never see her again.

You never even got to say goodbye.

••••••••●•••••••••

My head is a kite. My chest is on fire. My legs are filled with sand. It's so hard to move, but I have to keep going, find an escape, somewhere to hide, away from all the people who want to say, *It isn't your fault* and *You did your best* and *You should go home.* I blunder forward, one heavy foot after another. This hallway— when will it end? Soon, I expect. Sooner than I expect. That's the way of the world. Sure enough, there's a door. A sign: *Emergency Exit Only.* I push, like I pushed on Evie's chest. But just once. Not dozens of times. Not hundreds. An ache chews on my wrists as the door swings open. No bells or alarms. No siren. That's gone now. She went with it.

The sky. Bright blue. Full of sun. It's a lie, a trick. You know it's gray.

That's it, Munro—crush every stray leaf on the path. spit in the flower beds. See the signs up ahead? They don't have to tell you. You know where you're going.

There's no theater or tennis courts here like at DSS. No storage shed. There's just a house. A front door with the number 4 on it. It's locked. Doesn't matter—this is your hideout. It's quiet. Still. No one inside. Grab a rock from the pile near the mailbox and bring it back to the nearest window. Wrap it in your shirt. Smash the glass. Good. Now you're inside, where no one can find you.

Except me.

No thoughts. No feelings. Just heartache. And a stone in my throat that won't budge. The couch looks good. I ditch my bag. As I lie down, I feel pain in my right hand. I hold it up to my face. It's cut, bleeding. It could do with a bandage, but that wouldn't make it better.

All I want to do is sleep.

AWAY

Sunlight pours through the broken window. I rub my eyes and peek at my watch. Just after eight. In the morning. The day after. I look down to find my hand bandaged. The person responsible is packing up to leave.

"Perry?"

"Hello, Munro. I'm sorry I disturbed you."

"It's, um, fine. What...what are you doing here?"

"Kelvin sent me here. He said I needed to stop you bleeding to death. That's not a very good joke, because you were never in danger of bleeding to death. The wound is superficial. Jackie Chan has had much worse making his movies." He turns his head to the side and squints. "You are probably wondering why I bandaged you while you were unconscious. It's not good social skills to be in your personal space like that without you knowing, but I thought it might be easier and less painful that way because you were sleeping so deeply. I hope you are okay with that."

I hold up my dressed arm. "Didn't feel a thing. Thank you."

Perry wipes his hands on his thighs. "You're welcome. Do you mind if I ask you a question?"

"Is it why did I break into House 4 for the night?"

"Good guess! Why did you do that?"

"I wanted to be alone."

"Do you still want to be alone?"

I think for a moment. "No. I don't."

"That's good. We all need to be alone sometimes, but we also cannot live in a world of one. No lie." Perry looks at his watch. "I have to go and babysit my nephew now. I hope to see you this afternoon, Munro. Kelvin mentioned you might be staying here for a little while."

"Actually, I'll be out of here today. Then heading back to Vancouver, probably in the next day or two."

"I think your mum and dad will be very pleased to see you."

"For sure. Take care of your sister, eh."

Perry nods, then winks. "Take care of yourself."

He exits House 4.

·········●●·········

I stare at my phone for ten minutes. Old texts from Caro. Lou's Facebook page. A post he shared about the E-LIFE button campaign leads me to the Foundation's site. It looks unchanged from a week ago. Strange, I think. New content has been the standard since it went live, whether it's a blog entry or a video or a media release.

There are eleven missed calls on FaceTime, the last at six o'clock this morning. I sigh and look around the living room for a suitable place to surrender. The small table where Shah and I played checkess draws me over. I sit down and, making sure my bandaged hand is out of the picture, thumb the green icon.

The answer is almost immediate, two buzzes and connection. My parents fill the screen. They don't speak, don't even move. They're like wallpaper. I start talking.

"Mom, Dad…I'm sorry. I should have told you what I'd planned to do these last few weeks. A bunch of times I ditched school and headed out to Fair Go. I felt like I had to do it. I had to do more. For my team of residents. For me.

"It hasn't worked out—in fact, everything's gone to shit. I take full responsibility for that. And I know what the consequences are. I'm not ready to say goodbye, but…I guess no one ever is."

My parents turn to each other, brows lifted, sharing some mutual thought that won't be said. After a few seconds Dad removes his glasses and stares down the camera like a judge about to pass sentence.

"You done?"

"Yes."

"Nothing else you want to say?"

"I could say sorry again."

Dad holds up a hand. "Not necessary."

He looks to the side, as if off-camera a stranger has arrived and wants in on the discussion.

"Munro, do you ever talk to Evelyn?" he asks.

I glance at my bandaged hand. "Yeah. I do. Sometimes. She never answers."

Dad finds a thin smile that quickly shape-shifts into a grimace. "You know what? I talk to her too. Quite often. I talk about stuff that's happening now, good times from the past. About Mom, the Foundation. You. Every time I speak to her, I end up apologizing. *I'm sorry I wasn't there for you at the end, my sweet. I'm sorry I wasn't with you. I should've been with you.* Then a few weeks ago, I stopped mid-apology. A thought was in my head. I don't know if it just appeared on its own or if it had been there all along and finally found a way out. Maybe Evie put it there. However it happened, it socked me right in the jaw. The thought was, If my daughter had known when she was going to die, who would she have wanted there with her? Who would she have wanted by her side at the end?

"The answer was obvious—it was you, son. Of course it was you. Her big brother. The person who let her win at computer games and painted her bedroom every time she wanted to change the color. The person who showed her how to skate backward, and read *Treasure Island* to her. Her favorite person in the world. I realized after all this time that my apologies to Evelyn were selfish. I was wishing I'd been there for her when, truthfully, I was wishing I'd been there for *me*."

Dad's voice cracks on the final phrase. I try to swallow and fail. The heartbeats in my ears are weak and thin, like small sighs. I tell him there's no need to keep going. If there's more to say, he can tell me in person soon enough. He pulls himself together with another sideways look. Mom dabs her nose with a tissue and grasps his hand.

"We're here for you, son," he says. "Whenever you return."

I side-eye my phone, then give it a little shake. "*Whenever*?"

Mom nods. "That fellow from YOLO recommended that you come home, and we agreed. You should come home." She points. "*You*. The real you. Like we said last time, we can't bring you back. Only you can."

"And when you do," adds Dad, "there's a little Foundation idea we'd like your help with." He takes a photo out of his pocket and holds it up to the camera. It's a selfie. He and Mom standing in a vacant plot of land. There's a *FOR SALE!* sign between them.

"Five acres in Chilliwack," says Mom. "Future site of Evelyn Maddux Community Village."

"We're looking into it," corrects Dad.

I lean in, studying every detail of the image. "Is this for real?"

"Yes."

"You're thinking of buying this?"

"Like I said, we're looking into it."

"I don't know what to say."

"Say you'll work with us to make it happen one day."

"Are you kidding, Dad? I'll start working with you as soon as I step off the plane."

"Well, right now, focus on bringing Munro Maddux back." He grabs Mom's hand and kisses it. "Whenever."

I shut my eyes. In the absence of sight, House 4 speaks to my other senses. The air is stale, despite the broken window. The thin film of dust on the table coats my fingertips. The fridge *whirrs* away in the kitchen, dutifully keeping the tray of ice cubes cold. My mind shifts to Blake's house at Fair Go. Is it like this already? Is there any trace of her left? Any sign that she had a full, rich, loving life under its roof? I open my eyes.

"Mom, Dad, thank you for letting me stay," I reply. "But I think it's time to say goodbye to Fair Go."

..........●..........

"During Morning Connections I showed the team the text you sent me about quitting," says Kelvin, holding a sheet of plastic against the damaged window. I hand him a strip of duct tape. "They refused."

"Refused?"

"With extreme prejudice."

"What about Dale?"

"I didn't ask him. He's not in your team."

"Maybe not formally, but he is though. And his opinion—it's the one that really counts."

"More than the others?"

"The others have to accept my decision, Kelvin. It's *my* decision."

"They know it's your decision. They're just adamant it's the wrong one."

"Aw, man. It's not like I want to go. It's just…you know…I need to put their photos in the drawer."

"They don't agree, Munro. They believe there's still work to be done together. They want to finish the Straya Tour too."

"Haven't we seen everything in South East Queensland?"

"Apparently not."

I cut another strip of tape and hand it over. "Maybe I should just take off. I could do that."

He fastens the bottom edge of the plastic sheet. "It'd be hard on them. They're tough buggers though. They'll get over it. Eventually."

"How do I make them get over it *now*?" I watch him press against the plastic cover, testing its strength. I snap my fingers. "We'll put it to a vote, Dale included."

Kelvin wipes his hands, steps back and surveys his handiwork.

"I had a feeling you might say that."

......•......

The panel is done.

The votes are in.

Unlike my interview a lifetime ago, there's no Streets Ice Cream tub as ballot box. The residents agreed that the results didn't have to be kept secret. I think it was a show of respect to Dale. Everyone understands that if there's going to be a No, it'll be from him, and nobody will hold it against him. Me least of all.

Kelvin claps his hands. "Okay, looks like the people have spoken. Let's see what they said. As discussed, the question was, do you want Munro to stay? You needed to write your response down so it's on record. Each person will have a chance to share their response. You can show what you wrote too, if you like. You can add a brief comment, say why you voted the way you did. Keep it short…Bernie, I'm looking at you."

Kelvin pauses, fixing his gaze on me for a few seconds. I barely notice. My focus is on Dale. He's on his iPad, as he has been since he arrived. He hasn't spoken or made eye contact. From the *bleeps* and *bloops* coming from the device, I think he's playing a game. Kelvin continues.

"If there is a No vote cast this morning, Munro has assured me he will allow enough time to say goodbye. Righto, that's it for the gasbagging. Flo, how about you go first."

Florence holds up her paper and shows the group what she scribbled. It sort of looks like a little anchor and hook.

"You think Munro should go fishing?"

She looks at Kelvin like he could be used as bait. "This is Japanese. It says *hai*, which means yes in English. Munro should stay so I can keep usin' him in my class demos."

"Thanks for that, Flo. I'm sure he's looking forward to the next one. Iggy, you're up."

Iggy pulls his shoulders back and flips his card. He's done a drawing—a from-behind view of a super-hero standing legs apart, one hand on his hip, the other giving a raised thumb. On his cape is the word *YES*, surrounded by stars.

"Infecto will reveal himself to the world soon. Munro, you have to be here for it!"

"Nice piccie, Ig. Two Yes votes. Bernadette?"

Bernie blinks twice and snaps her fingers. "I vote Yes, mostly because Munro is a great Living Partner and a very good friend and I want to see his face many more times before his exchange is finished and he truly has to leave. I also want him to help me design some more caps, ones that might appeal to Canadians."

Kelvin does a double take. "That's it?"

"That's it."

"Wow, regardless of the outcome, we've achieved a little history this morning. Bernie ended a speech before our ears fell off."

"You're such a goose, Kelvin."

"You can put that on a cap for me. Well, that just leaves…Dale. Over to you, pal."

Dale rises. Though he is the center of attention, he keeps his head down, continues his scrutiny of the iPad. I can't tell what he's feeling right now. It better not be guilt. No guilt allowed, bud. You've got nothing to feel bad about. He presses down on the volume button, increasing it to somewhere near max. His fingers begin to skitter along the screen.

This vote, it's a combined one. From me and Blake.

There's a gasp from the panel. I'm not sure who coughed it up. Dale, gaze still averted, waits for any hint of dissent. We're all too stunned to process, let alone protest. Kelvin steps forward, thumbs hooked into his belt loops.

"Mate, you're saying this is how Blake would've voted if she were here?"

Fingers dance.

She is here.

I pivot toward the Rec Refuge entrance, genuinely hoping to see a dramatic, movie-like reveal. The door stays shut.

After Morning Connections I messaged Blake on Facebook. Told her about the vote. She wanted in. She's

snuck on to a computer at her house. She's waiting for me to let her know what happened.

Kelvin shrugs. "I guess if nobody has any objections..."

Dale comes around the table, stopping an arm's length in front of me. He's wearing a new shirt, a yellow polo with the Billabong wave on the pocket. Fitting— a wave for a goodbye. Still no eye contact. Maybe it's for the best.

He taps the screen and the iPad voice says, **Dearly beloved, we are gathered here today at the Rec Refuge to decide if Munro Maddux—Canadian citizen, high school exchange student, Living Partner and the dude responsible for the Boggo Road wedding—should never come back to Fair Go. If anyone knows why Munro should be allowed to stay without this vote being shown, speak now or forever shut your gob.**

Bernie shoots her hand into the air. Kelvin scurries over, has a quiet word in her ear. She lowers her hand.

Munro, do you take Fair Go to still be your home away from home? Do you promise to keep assisting with our projects and finish the Straya Tour and help us get better at floor hockey? Do you promise to be the best "brother" to us you can be, even though you will return to Vancouver for real at the end of August?

Do you promise to bring Caro back here before you go, because we really like her and we think you would make an excellent couple? And, most of all, do you promise to never, ever, EVER feel bad about giving Blake and Dale their once-in-a-lifetime chance to be together, now and forever?

He lifts his head and stares at me, bushy eyebrows arched, tongue buried in his cheek. His hand "yaps"— a gesture for me to respond.

"I…do?"

By the power vested in me, I now pronounce the vote of Blake and Dale to be Yes. You may now shake my hand.

I hesitate, unsure what's happening. Dale ups the ante and pulls me into a bear hug. The others cheer and applaud and bang on the table. He releases me while I splutter the only words in my jumbled brain that haven't been mown down by light-speed shock.

"Dale, you…you and Blake…you *aren't* together."

He scoffs.

Of course we are! Okay, my girl doesn't live here anymore, and that makes me sad sometimes. But that doesn't change what we said to each other at Boggo Road. It doesn't change us.

"But her dad…he doesn't want Blake to see you anymore."

Fuck that guy.

A new round of cheers and table banging. Dale turns to them and raises the roof.

He can't stop us being together forever. Dale points to his chest. **He can't stop this.**

"No, he can't."

Word. By the way, do you have something in your eye, Munro Maddux?

"It's a bit dusty in here."

Dale shows me the iPad screen. Blake's Facebook DM is up. There are more raised thumbs and happy faces and love hearts than I can count.

"Righto then," announces Kelvin. "It appears we have a unanimous verdict. Now, finish this sentence, Kid Canuck. Sometimes life—"

"Takes on a life of its own," I reply, the words rolling off my tongue.

·············●············

Caro is sitting on the curb by the Fair Go front-entrance sign.

As I approach her, questions pile on top of one another like cards in a game of Snap. What are you doing here? How did you know I was still here? Do you not believe in goodbyes? Did you somehow figure out

I'm staying? No doubt she's got a few queries too, not the least of which is probably *What's with the bandage on your hand?* All of them go unasked. I drop my bag on the dry grass and sit next to her as the sun slips behind a bank of dark clouds in the west. A flash of far-off sheet lightning triggers a low, lazy grumble of thunder. It prompts a memory. There was a downpour the night we rode together in the taxi. Stormy weather at the beginning and at the end.

Only this isn't the end.

"Just before Evie died, I was teaching her to ride a bike," I begin. "I always made sure she didn't fall. I'd put my left hand over hers on the handlebars and my right on the back of her seat. She'd push on the pedals and I'd run beside her, keeping a firm grip, ready to squeeze the brake if she went too fast. Evie always complained, *I can do this! I can stay up by myself! Stop holding on to me, Munro! Let go!*"

"*Soon*, I'd say. *Just a little more time.* And I'd grip the handlebars and the seat a bit tighter. I suspect she was right. She could've ridden on her own. But she never did."

I stop for a second, trying to get some saliva back in my mouth. Then I lie back on the grass, bringing my hands to my head. A wide black blanket of fruit bats squeaks and squabbles as it arcs through the dusky sky. Caro stays seated, cross-legged, facing me.

"When Evie collapsed, I let go of her. She was walking beside me, holding my right hand, then *boom!* She dropped like a stack of bricks. I held on for a second, maybe two. I was afraid of falling on top of her, hurting her. That's the lie I told myself afterward. For a while anyway. Later, I wondered if letting go meant I couldn't revive her. Did I break some crucial connection we had? If I'd stayed with her the whole way down, would that connection have been saved? Would her *life* have been saved? I've told Evie I'm sorry so many times. *I'm sorry I let you go.* She never answers."

Tears spill from the corners of my eyes and scoot toward the dry ground. Caro's shadow falls across much of my upper body. It sways and quivers.

"I don't think I'll ever totally get over it. But I think I'm ready to get through it." I sit up. "Can you get over me ditching on Vaccination Day?"

She laughs. She says she has to because I now know what an ugly crier she is. Not a good look for a kick-ass lawyer.

"By the way," I add, "forget the closing argument for my goodbye. I'm not going home now. I'm staying. Till the end of the exchange."

Caro is perfectly still for a moment, and then she launches herself at me. We roll around and grab at each other, the baked grass crunching beneath our bodies.

We kiss. Somewhere in the tangle, my right hand takes hold of hers.

On the horizon, thunder pounds, like a single, long, strong heartbeat.

·········●·········

When I knock on the Hydes' front door, all three answer.

"Omigod, Munro," says Nina, wrapping herself around me with Kraken-like limbs. "I'm so glad you're back. We were worried. Not frantic—we knew where you were—but still worried. Why didn't you use your key to get in? Did you lose it? What happened to your hand? Are you hurt? Do we need to take you to the doctor? Geordie, call Doctor Hallinan. Are you staying here now? Or are you staying at Fair Go for a bit? We want you here, but we understand if you need more time. Geordie can drive you there."

"Other Mother," I reply, "that's a lot to take in. I think 'I'm here and I'm good' probably covers everything."

The trio shepherds me into the kitchen. Nina, Geordie and I sit on the stools. Rowan hoists himself onto the island.

"Row showed us your text," says Geordie. "We're rapt you're not going home just yet, mate."

"You sure about that? I lied to you guys. I sneaked around behind your backs. I made your son an accessory."

"No doubt you had to twist his arm."

"I wouldn't blame you if you called it quits. Honestly."

Geordie pats the left side of his chest. "We're not pulling up stumps, but we do expect a medal for our bravery."

"You deserve one."

"The look you've got on your face right now, champ…that's enough."

"I'm going to cook a pav tonight to celebrate that look," adds Rowan.

I feel heat in my cheeks and forehead. "Thank you. You guys are amazing. There hasn't been much to celebrate to this point. But I'm going to be at my best from now on." I drape an arm over each Hyde parent and draw them close. "How do you feel about having a perfect exchange student the rest of the way? It'll be just like a video on the YOLO website. Let's call it *No More Down Under Achiever.*"

••••••••●•••••••••

My bedroom. Minus last night, my final place of rest for the past hundred days. My final place of rest for the next hundred.

Mister Koala is still beside the alarm clock. He didn't move during my absence. Clearly, he wasn't concerned.

He knew I'd be back. And he kept himself busy with the job he was assigned to do. I give him a small salute, then pick him up in my left hand. With my right, I lift the black pawn from his grip.

I unzip the top pocket of my empty suitcase. Evie's ruby-red ribbon—tied to the handle when I made the trip over—is coiled so it looks like a tiny nest. I drop the chess piece in and close the pocket.

You're not going home after all, Munro.

Not today, Coyote. Not tomorrow.

You're here for the whole exchange.

I am.

Then you go home.

Then I go home. Me.

Is this where we part ways? Where we say goodbye?

I think it is.

Munro?

Yes?

Your father was right.

About what?

Evie wanted you by her side. At the end.

THE LAST TIME

Familiar landmarks rush by. Houses on stilts. Beer bill-boards. The golf course. An abandoned trailer. Coal cars covered in graffiti. I can almost close my eyes and know where I am and what comes next. Forget what comes next—I want to be in this moment for as long as possible.

"We've sold over two hundred now."

I turn away from the window and pat Caro on the knee. "Sorry?"

She taps the E-LIFE button on her purse. "Two hundred and seventeen sold, to be exact. In just four weeks."

"Wow. That's amazing. You're amazing."

"It's not just me, Munro."

"I know, I know. Renee and Maeve and Digger are amazing too."

"You forgot about Rowan."

"He's an asshole."

"Munro!"

"Kidding!"

Caro gives me a small shove and worms an arm around my elbow. "Dig's going to ask Jessica Mauboy to the semiformal tomorrow."

"Tomorrow?"

"He figures five months' notice is more than enough."

"I guess. Is there still a whole thing planned for it?"

Caro nods. "After he sends the tweet, we're all going to watch a movie together. *Forgetting Sarah Marshall* or *She's Out of My League*. One of those. Rowan's going to cook us all dinner." Caro arches an eyebrow. "Are you going to come?"

"Sure."

"I don't want you doing it just for me."

I laugh. "Full of yourself, aren't you, Ms. Wakefield? I'll be there on behalf of the Foundation, to say thank you to the gang for all their hard work. And *She's Out of My League* just happens to be my favorite film of all time."

"Oh, really? It's knocked *Mad Max: Fury Road* out of number one?"

"*She's Out of My League* has better stunts."

Caro bursts out laughing. She snuggles up to my shoulder as I tune back in to the Brisbane landscape coasting past the window. Wooden fences. Rugby fields. A car-repair business called Dent Doctor.

"I think you're going to miss riding this train when you go home, Munro."

I note the glum look accompanying the words. "Hey, it's only June. There's still two and a half months left in the exchange. That's a lifetime."

"Lifetimes go quick."

"Not always."

"You think we'll stay together when this 'lifetime' is over?"

"Why not? Thunder always follows lightning."

"I thought I was the lightning."

"Nah, you're the Thunder. From Down Under."

Caro rolls her eyes and pretend gags. "One monthiversary," she says. "Doesn't feel like we've been going out for that long. Feels a lot longer."

"I'll take that as a compliment."

"I've booked us into a great place tonight. Liber8. Top atmosphere, really chill. You're gonna love it."

I remove Caro's smirk with a tickling barrage. She squeals and bucks and threatens to use the Kookaburra Laugh on me. She doesn't get the chance—the train starts slowing down, and the automated PA message tells us our stop is next.

·······●●●········

Kelvin hands me a present. I tear open the wrapping.

"The official Munro Maddux Straya Tour DVD and T-shirt," he says. "It's not what we're putting up on the site. This is a special director's cut, just for you. About fifteen minutes long."

I hand the DVD to Caro and examine the shirt. All the tour dates and destinations are printed on the back, twelve stops in total. Bribie Island figures twice. Boggo Road is there.

"Want to watch the video?"

"Have we got time?" she asks.

"We have. The guys aren't looking to get started just yet."

The title hits the TV screen, and the first frames show the bus door opening wide. Kelvin, sitting in the driver's seat, turns to the camera and points. "Munro Maddux...this is for you from all of us!"

Footage rolls, starting with the trip to South Bank, followed by snippets from the rest of the tour. Expected moments of awesomeness dominate—Flo-jitsu lessons, SNAP reminders, sketchbook scribbling—but there are surprises too. Long wigs mimicking my hair. A *Three Things I Love About My Living Partner* survey. Karaoke of "O Canada." Discussion about who would win a fight between me and Justin Bieber (I'm the unanimous pick). Then there are the gut punchers. Dale and Blake at the beach, her head on his shoulder. Shah sleeping on the bus, soccer ball in his lap. All the action is paced by Aussie music from Kelvin's bus playlists—Tame Impala, Hilltop Hoods, Dick Diver, Alison Wonderland, Daniel Johns.

Despite several chin wobbles and breath catches, I manage to keep it together. Caro doesn't even try. She sniffs and sighs and fusses with her eyes from the first image to the last. Fair Go has found a little corner of her heart as well. I'm guessing she'll keep coming here after I leave.

"What'd you think of that?" asks Kelvin, replacing the DVD in its case.

"Loved every second."

"Favorite moments?"

"All the shots of me walking side by side with the guys."

"Nice. Anything you would like to have seen that wasn't on there?"

I exhale hard. "The wedding. The games of checkess."

Kelvin nods. "You want to leave this stuff here until you go?"

"Sure."

"Righto then!" Kelvin claps his hands. "Let's see what these guys have planned for you, young fella!"

...........●..........

"We wanted to party," says Bernie, straddling the Shed's closest sideline, "because the Straya Tour is finished, and because this is the last time we'll be together like this."

Caro winds an arm around my waist, sensing I might need a bit of propping up.

"The last time?" I ask.

"Correct. The group won't be the same after today."

"How come?"

"Us four—the team that's left from the Straya Tour—we'll be five tomorrow."

"A new resident is moving in!" says Iggy.

To House 4, adds Dale.

"That's right. A stranger. Someone we've never met before. So we wanted to make today special. Just for us."

I scan the group and swallow hard. "Man, I love you guys." Faces beam. Eyes glint. "Here's to us. The last time."

Kelvin clears his throat. "Okay, this is supposed to be a party, not a Harlequin romance. Let's get it started!"

Bernie launches into Pink's song and disappears into the storeroom. She returns dragging the Bauer bags.

"Floor hockey, my fellow Freetards?"

For almost an hour, we play three on three with scorers being subbed out. Then I throw on the goalie gear for one last shootout. I get beat glove side, blocker, five-hole—not all of them are whiffs. Quite a few are quality shots. The team's improved a ton since the first session. And the progress will continue: Bernie says lunchtime floor-hockey games will start soon. Peer-to-peer training of the other residents is in the works. Iggy adds that he wants to learn the art of goaltending and take owner-ship of the equipment. Making saves like a superhero, like Infecto. He's all over that.

As we pack up the bags, Kelvin brings a cake out on a cart. It's in the shape of Australia. In the center are two fondant figures—a bottle of Bundaberg rum and a bottle of Coke. The writing on the cake says *A Good Time, Not A Long Time.*

"Rowan from your host family put it together," says Kelvin. "His dad, Geordie, dropped it off last night. He assured me there's no rum in it."

We slice it up and hand it around. I'm face deep in a second helping of South East Queensland when Caro touches me on the shoulder.

"You okay?"

"Yeah."

"You're all pale. And sweaty."

"The guys were awesome in the game. Got my heart going, for sure."

"They seem to be pretty good at that." Caro smiles and notes the time. "I'm heading off now. I need time to make myself gorgeous for tonight."

"Two minutes is all you need." Caro says I'm sweet, then brushes away the crumbs I sprayed on her shirt.

"You want to come?" she asks.

I look around the Shed, then at the walkway leading to the outside. "Think I'll stick around. Just for a bit longer."

Caro nods, and we kiss. Dale fires up the iPad:

AWW YEAH!

"Don't be too long," she says, placing her hand on my cheek. "Don't make me come and get you."

••••••••●•••••••

The Creative Arts Precinct, the Digital Media Center, the Agriculture Precinct, the Rec Refuge, the Recycling Depot, the kitchen, the cafeteria. I imagine each one lifted up, carried across the ocean and set down on the Chilliwack land. I see Evie looking them over. Though I can't hear her voice, I know she would want changes. Nicer plants. Bigger chairs. Wooden floors out. Thick carpet in. Less white. More ruby red. I can actually visualize her as a resident too. Is it because the Coyote's gone?

Or because the sign at the front entrance would bear her name. Or because she would be right at home among the Bernies and the Florences and the Iggys and the Dales living there. I don't know. Maybe all of the above.

At the central intersection in Fair Go, signs pointing the separate ways, Bernie breaks the silence. "Is there anywhere else you want to go, Munro?"

I look toward House 4, with its palm trees and its welcome mat and its long windows. The small patio out front and the gentle ramp down the side.

"One more thing."

I haven't seen the place since my overnight stay. It's alive again. The dust is gone. The air has a lemony scent. Everything from floor to ceiling has been given a scrub. Scuffs and marks and old fingerprints have vanished—in their place are bright patterns and gleaming surfaces. A fish tank with four residents sits on the sideboard.

"Looks like it's ready," I say.

Bernie nods. "We are too."

"Freetard cap on the hatstand? Nice."

"I thought it would be a good welcoming present. You think so?"

"Definitely."

The front door creaks. Soft, swishy footsteps float down the hall. I look at the others, brow crinkled.

"It's just us, Kelvin," I say. "Don't worry—we're not messing up the place. Kelvin?"

"Who you talkin' to?" asks Florence.

"You all right?" adds Iggy. "You don't look so good."

I breathe through dry lips, unable to calm myself with a count. I look around house 4. It's suddenly different. Far away. Off in the distance. Blurred background for the surprise visitor.

"Evie?" I whisper.

My head dips. It stays down, my short-circuiting eyes staring at my sternum. A grunt pushes out of my mouth. My heart is in a vice. I feel shooting pain in my hand. My left, not my right. My feet crumble. I fall.

And it is Evie I see. She kneels beside me. She's just as I hoped she'd be. Ski-jump nose. Pixie ears. Big tongue. Eyes the color of Kalamalka Lake. The ribbon in her caramel hair is ruby red. Same color as her lips.

She listens for breathing.

She checks for a pulse.

She starts to press on my chest.

THE END

Are you there?

Yes.

I can't see you now.

No. But you can hear me.

Is it really you, Evie?

It's me.

Not the Coyote?

The Coyote is gone, Munro.

Where's the team? Are they okay?

They're fine.

You sure?

Cross my heart, hope to die.

Not funny. Where are we?

You're here.

Where's *here*?

Where you are now.

I don't like it here.

I figured.

I'm supposed to be meeting up with Caro. It's our one monthiversary. She'll be waiting. I have to go.

You can't.

Why not?

Because you need to stay.

For how long?

Until you get better.

This is bullshit, Evie. I got better already. Now I have to do it again?

Sometimes Life takes on a life of its own.

You heard Kelvin say that.

No, I heard you say that.

I don't want to die, Evie.

Everyone has to die.

I mean, I don't want to die now.

I know.

The Coyote's probably waiting for me.

Things are different now, Munro. You can hear me. If he tries to mess with you again, I'll give him the Kookaburra Laugh.

Yeah?

Of course! Someone has to watch out for you and protect you.

True dat.

Okay, I have to go now, but I have a present for you. It's next to you. Do you like it?

Another squirrel tie?

No, it's the one I gave you for grad. You should put it on tonight for Caro.

But you said I can't leave here!

Just take it, okay?

Thank you, Evie.

You're welcome.

Hey, Evie?

Yes?

I'm sorry I let you go.

You didn't.

I'm not talking about when I was teaching you to ride a bike.

Neither am I.

I'm so sorry, Evie.

Don't be. I'm glad we were together then. I'm glad we're together now.

Talk to you soon, little sister.

Right back atcha, big brother.

I love you.

I love you too.

Goodbye.

REST IN PEACE

"Hello."

I open my eyes a fraction. The light muscles in, grinding on my vision like sandpaper. I blink in double time.

"You were away for a bit there."

The scene softens. Watery blurs begin to take shape and find definition. I'm in a bed. A machine with numbers and graphs stands to my right. Under it are white boxes and blue bins. To my left are tubes, thick and thin, going up, going down. One tracks into my nose, another into my arm. Wires are stuck to my chest.

"So glad to have you back."

Anxious faces surround me. The Hydes. Caro. Kelvin.

My team.

I dig my elbows into the mattress and attempt to shift. A volcano erupts in my chest.

"Whoa there, champ," says Kelvin. "You gotta take it easy."

I try to speak. The words are too brittle to come out in one piece. Dale pushes through to the edge of the bed. He hands me his iPad. I touch the screen. Each movement is like a match being struck on my ribs.

You're all here.

Kelvin hikes a thumb over his shoulder. "They told us only two at a time, but we told them to get stuffed. Then they told us visitors limited to family. We told them we are the family until your folks arrive. And to get stuffed."

Parents.

Nina steps forward. "They're on their way, Munro. Flight lands in a few hours. Geordie's going to pick them up and bring them straight to the hospital. They're staying with us." She begins to well up. Geordie pulls her close. "They know you're okay, Munro."

I fell.

Kelvin surveys the others, then nods. "You collapsed. Doc gave us the story. Your heart's a bit out of whack."

A hole?

"What's that?"

Is there a hole in my heart?

"No, no hole. Doc thinks it may have sustained some damage a while back. Stopped it pumping properly. You had any chest pains, shortness of breath, light-headedness, that sort of stuff?"

Only the last fifteen months.

"Well, that's probably how long you've had a heart problem. Doc called it some fancy name. Hyperactive, hyperbolic…cardiosomething-or-other."

Fuck.

"It's okay. Thanks to our mate Iggy, you got the jump start you needed. And it's not a permanent thing. Doc said it's treatable. Things will go back to normal."

I take a deep breath. Not a good idea.

Iggy did CPR?

Florence releases Iggy's hand and urges him forward.

You saved my life, Ig.

He blushes and puffs out his chest. Then he gets into a stance. "I'm a good goaltender."

Tired laughter flits through the room. Rowan speaks as it dies away. "I brought you something. Caro suggested I get it from home and bring it here." He points at the safety bar by my right hand. I scrabble around, grab the object hanging on the bar. With gritted teeth, I bring it up to my eyeline.

The squirrel tie.

Put it on me.

"You think that's wise?" asks Rowan.

Please.

"Okay then. Promise I'll be really gentle."

Not you. Caro.

Rowan huffs. "Typical."

He hands over the tie. Caro's different from this morning, different from any other time I've seen her. Her hair is pulled back into a long braid. The black wristbands are gone. Her nails are bright yellow. She's a sight for sore eyes. And hearts. Caro leans in and presses her cheek to mine. She cradles the back of my head in her hand.

"You made me come and get you," she whispers.

She kisses me and withdraws. The tie is looped around my neck and laid out on my upper body, covering the wires on my chest.

Kelvin raises a hand. "Um, Munro, the residents have asked for five minutes alone with you. Is that cool?"

Of course.

The Hydes exit, pledging to be "back in a tick." Kelvin is on his phone before he reaches the door. Caro squeezes my right hand and follows him out. There's a minor commotion outside the room and down the hall. The door shuts, and quiet resumes.

Noise?

"People from your school," says Bernie. "A few teachers, some students. They asked me how you were feeling."

What did you say?

"I told them you are feeling like a Freetard. Then I told them where they could get my exclusive Freetard shirts and hats."

Perfect.

The foursome moves closer, crowding the bed. They look beat, but not freaked. Tough buggers. I offer Dale his iPad. He gestures for me to keep using it.

So glad you're here.

"The hospital wanted us to talk to a counselor," says Iggy. "I said I wanted to talk to you."

Stop it.

"You're in a lot of pain," he adds.

I can handle it.

"I drew a picture of Infecto for you while you were sleeping." He holds up the sketch and shoves it in my face. "I made the outfit just like you said at South Bank. Skintight yellow suit. Cape made of wipes. I did the skull and crossbones instead of a petri dish—I like that better. And she's got the platinum mask with the germs on it."

I thought Infecto was a guy?

"I changed him to a girl."

She looks like somebody we know.

I turn my head toward Florence. She's standing at the foot of the bed. Her pose matches Iggy's drawing—legs apart, arms folded.

Thumb-wrestle.

"What?"

Right hand. Right now.

Florence smirks and cracks her knuckles. "Finally! I thought you were just gonna lay there all day like a goanna in the sun."

"Before you do that and get crushed, Munro," says Bernie, "we need to vote. Actually, *you* need to vote." She pulls her shoulders back and lifts her chin. "We didn't know your heart was sick. We would've skipped the floor hockey. Or told Caro to take you to Emergency. Or called the ambulance instead of eating cake. It would be great if we could have a do-over, but we can't. Do-over—that's one of your Canadian words, isn't it?"

I start working the iPad. Bernie holds up her hand. **S is for stop.** "You may never want to think about how your heart stopped today," she says. "Because of that, you might not want to see us again. Or hear from us or talk to us. You might want to leave and never come back. And we would be sad if you did. But we have lots of great memories. So there is a question we have to ask. And you need to vote, yes or no."

Bernie looks to the others. They nod in agreement.

"Do you still want to be our Living Partner?"

I scan the hopeful faces, then type.

To make the right choice, I must listen to the voice inside my head.

"What's it saying?" asks Iggy.

I tap the screen.

HELL NO HELL NO HELL NO HELL NO HELL NO HELL NO HELL NO HELL NO

I bring my right hand up to my chest. Despite the agony, laughs come. Real ones, not programmed from the iPad.

"Actually, we were just being nice," says Bernie. "You don't get a vote." She gives me a gentle fist bump. Three more fist bumps follow. "Okay then," she adds, "we should go now because you probably need to sleep again." She turns to Florence. "Don't worry—you can crush Munro in the morning."

Morning.

"We're ditching," says Iggy.

I gingerly lift my arm and wag a finger. I go to hand the iPad back to Dale. He leans over, types and stabs the screen: **Keep it until you can talk again. I've got another.**

The team says one last goodbye, waves, then exits. Before the door can shut behind them, a nurse bustles in.

He's tanned and blond and has biceps like bowling balls. He looks like Whistler material.

"You're awake, Munro!" he says.

Only just.

"You got a vocal aid there? Nice!" He takes a closer look. I read his name tag.

You gotta be shitting me.

"Hey?"

Your name is Wiley?

"Yep. Grant Wiley, Super Nurse."

Wiley. As in Coyote.

"Spot on. That was actually my nickname in high school." Grant Wiley checks my pulse, takes my blood pressure. After some chart scribbling, he folds his bulky arms and smiles. "Not bad, young fella. Now, you feeling chilly at all? Need an extra blanket or two?"

I'm good.

"Righto. I probably don't need to tell you to take it easy, but...no star jumps, no one-arm push-ups. No bench-pressing the bed."

I'll resist the urge.

"Right on. It's going to take you a little while to feel like yourself again, Munro. You'll need to stick around here for a bit, get better. Just until you're good enough to go home." Grant Wiley claps his hands once. "Sound like a plan?"

I turn off the iPad and open my mouth. My voice is weak and scratchy. But it's definitely mine.

"I can do that."

·············●············

Visiting hours are done. My "family" has left for the night. Grant Wiley is checking on other patients. It's my room now. My place of rest. Not the final one.

Sleep is calling. My eyelids are heavy. The room is already unconscious; only the quiet hum of the machines and shallow huff of the tubes remain. As I start to drift, an object on the windowsill makes a final impression— my koala buddy. I don't remember anyone saying they brought him to the hospital. And I don't remember anyone admitting they put a ruby-red ribbon in his outstretched arms. Maybe my eyes are playing tricks? Maybe I'm seeing things that aren't there?

That's okay. My hearing is just fine.

ACKNOWLEDGMENTS

The writing of this tale was, at times, Darren vs. the Novel. Fortunately, I had a lot of great family, friends, colleagues and Google searches in my corner. I'd like to thank my beautiful wife and first reader, Wend; my wondrous twins, Chloe and Jared; the Groths; the Frasers; my peerless, fearless editor, Sarah Harvey, and the Orca team; my splendid Oz publisher, Zoe Walton, and the Penguin Random House gang; my invaluable agents, Tara Wynne and John Pearce; Aaron Cully Drake; the End Crew of Patrick, Lauren and Julie; Youngcare; Bittersweet Farms; 2011 flood hero Chris Skehan; and all the young, special people I ever had the privilege of teaching.

ABOUT THE AUTHOR

Darren Groth is the author of six novels, including *Kindling* and the acclaimed YA novel *Are You Seeing Me?* He was the winner of the 2016 Adelaide Festival Award for Young Adult Literature and has been a finalist in numerous other prestigious prizes, including the CBCA Book of the Year (Australia), the Prime Minister's Literary Awards (Australia), the Governor General's Literary Awards (Canada) and the Sakura Medal (Japan).

Darren is a former special-education teacher and the proud father of a son with autism spectrum disorder (ASD). For fun, he watches *Game of Thrones* with his beautiful Canadian wife and eats at Fatburger with his wondrous sixteen-year-old twins. He lives in Vancouver, British Columbia. For more information, visit www.darrengroth.com.